D1325149

Sally's Road

A Novelette

A Fiction?

Jon Elkon

SALLY'S ROAD is the story of a woman dying of cancer, stuck in a bewilderingly soulless estate of modern houses in the stagnant backwaters of Shropshire where the sound of lawnmowers is the only confirmation of human habitation. Sally's grindingly boring life is changed complettely when she meets Annie - a tousled, tomboyish teenager who is tangled up in her own story of kidnap, murder and brothers called Peverill. When Annie tumbles over the fence two lives are in the balance....

"Black humour at its best"

ISBN-13: 978-1470140243
ISBN-10:1470140241

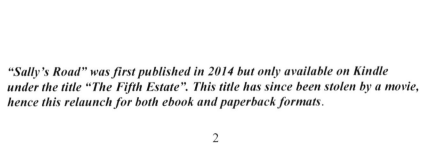

"Sally's Road" was first published in 2014 but only available on Kindle under the title "The Fifth Estate". This title has since been stolen by a movie, hence this relaunch for both ebook and paperback formats.

For Auntie Pam. Sorry.

SUNDAY

Dear Graham,

It is only fair that I send you this, my Journal, my misery memoir, my Cancer Diary, my Dice with Death so that you can find out why the tabloids will soon be describing me as a murderer, a rapist and a thief. You are, after all someone who has had a great impact on my life. I also realise that you did love me, and heaven knows, perhaps you still do.

But you must learn what kind of person I am so that you will stop blaming yourself and can go on to live a happy, useful life, giving your great love and kindness to someone who really deserves it.

Oh dear, what will the neighbours say...!

Do what you will with this book of horrors. It's yours.

Sorry, but I'm not.

Love

Sally.

BOOK I

CHAPTER ONE

The clatter or grind of lawnmowers and the silence of church bells. Sunday, and no bells. There were always bells in Bristol. I used to hate them so much. Once, Barry and I were so incensed (this was a Friday evening mind you, not a Sunday-morning-get-up-you-Christians, just some jolly morons on an irk-you regime) that we nailed a letter to the Church door. It said something like (I wish I could remember it) 'Your insensitivity and selfishness proves that you have completely forgotten the message of your founder...' etc...You know what? It seemed, after that, as if someone - possibly God - had taken notice because the bells were never quite as bad again.

Here in Spireslea one is safe from bells. They build these places as far away as possible from anything remotely resembling civilisation, though the village nearby - a crumbling Conservation Area with mouldy Georgian and half-timbered houses, a pub, a newsagent - I must stop being so cynical - is really rather lovely.

So why the hell can't we live *there*!

Instead of which here I am trussed up like a chicken in a party frock, all frills and pink bows and nowhere to go...

Hello dear Journal. Welcome to Spireslea! To the Redwood Way, to be precise, somewhere in the Midlands (I must Google map it. I'm told you can get aerial photographs). The nearest 'town' - if it is that - is Telford, a nightmare of chrome, glass and mass-produced factories - one of which employs my new husband. Who is asleep right now. It is nine am, and he will be asleep for another hour or two. I find this irritating.

I find quite a lot of things about Graham irritating.

I'm bursting to write everything down all at once! It seems ages since I've had someone to talk to, and I've only been here six weeks. I haven't made any friends on the Estate yet, and doubt if I will. Though I have managed to glean quite a lot about my neighbours. There's a small bespectacled garrulous man in the Post Office - I can never remember his name, which is embarrassing - who seems to think that I am some kind of fellow spirit, that I'm interested in my neighbours' banal lives.

There goes a Local! I can just see a stretch of road from the patio, and I caught a glimpse of Joan Bellings, stumping up the road as if she has somewhere to go. She's dressed in Countrywoman gear, massive knit, tweed skirt. Even from here she looks grubby, a Dickens character, sort of Aunt Pegotty of the Stews. The Newsagent fellow tells me she's from farming stock, upper-class farming stock. When he says this he taps the side of his nose. I wish I knew what that gesture means.

There are more locals awake next-door, I can hear the kids screaming. They're called the Melds. Margaret Meld is the woman, Roger the husband, I don't know the children's' names. Roger gets drunk, beats her up on Saturday nights - I presume it's some sort of prelude to sex - it's a ritual, anyway, and the noise no longer bothers me.

Besides, the PO Man reports that when she comes in for her papers on the Sunday mornings, she is always beaming and charming, despite obvious bruising. What a bastard! There are one or two benefits, I suppose, in my having married someone who at least <u>tries</u> to be a New

Man. I suppose being bored to death most of the time is a small price to pay.

Next-door, on the other side, are the Tweeds. (I'm making all these names up, by the way, in case this Journal is ever read by anybody. I don't really want to be cruel, after all.) Jean Tweed is quite another kettle of fish. She is always dressed up, I bet she goes to bed in her makeup - blood-painted lips, eyebrows plucked savagely, eyeliner saying He That Looks Me in the Eye Shall Die - I bumped into her at the PO when I went to pay for the papers fifteen or so minutes ago (when I saw you, dear Journal, fell in love and bought you right away. I hope I can keep up this writing a little each day resolution! I will try, I promise). I mean physically bumped into, didn't see her as I opened the door, she actually Harrumphed at me and shook her head - her mind saying, no doubt, these mannerless Provincials! She has a husband and daughter, I believe. While I can hear them sometimes, I have never seen either of them.

The other neighbour I know a little about is Harry Frost, a stereotype ex-army Major - who, PO Man tells me, was actually a *sergeant* major, which is something quite different. PO Man thinks this very funny indeed.

*

Spireslea is less a place, more a state of mind. In which tiny variations on the theme are badges of individuality, proudly trumpeted in the house descriptions. '...features a double bedroom with *en-suite,* tastefully accented in shades of burgundy and beige'... '...this Midland Dream Home is our top-of the range, with exquisite details including a faux-marble fireplace and hardwood decking to an expanse of luscious lawn (at the discretion of the Buyer'...which translates as some planks outside the back door and 30ft of rubble-laden soil which could, after many sweaty Sundays, become lawn.

More extracts from the brochure of Midland Dreamhomes plc. Slogan 'Home is where we make it': Poetry!

THE BLANDFORD
Planned with the modern family in mind, this supremely elegant three bedroom home offers truly luxurious living for all the family. With its attractive Georgian-style front door, full gas-fired central heating and superb appointments, this house is a dream home at an incredibly fair price.

Blandfords are the bottom of the range, and are now going for around one hundred and twenty thousand or less, Poman says. (I think I'll call him Poman. I like that. You know who I mean.)

The mid-range home is, of course, 'even more luxurious'. It has four bedrooms for a start, and the lounge is eighteen foot long, while the Blandford's is a mere sixteen.

THE CUMBRIA
This is a home for gracious living. It is built to the standards of quality you expect from Midland Dreamhomes plc, builders of beautiful homes for over six years. The house is lavishly equipped, and boasts full wall-to-wall carpets and a fully fitted kitchen with every luxury the devoted home-maker could demand...

The Cumbria, I am told, sells for around a hundred and fifty thousand these days. (A hundred and seventy when they were built in those pre-recession days!)

Ah, but the home all Estatemented Beings aspire to is the Top of the Range house, the Number One, the Cream-in-the-panties job -

THE PORTNOY

This is the top of the range house, the home dreams are made on...from its real-wood fitted kitchen to the Cream of Tomato matching bathroom suite, the PORTNOY offers the ultimate in luxury to the discerning home buyer. The stunning twenty-foot lounge is brilliantly shown off in the light of French windows that open onto a 40 foot garden with the potential to become the envy of all your friends...

Joan Bellings lives in a Blandford. The Tweeds live in a Cumbria. Major Frost's is...um...a Blandford.

Graham bought us a Portnoy and I will never forgive him for that. Bastard! For those six figures (he won't tell me the actual numbers, New Man or not) we could so easily have been snuggled up in an ivied thatched cottage with roses. 'Far too corny!' He says. 'Think of the maintenance! The repairs! The dry rot! The wet rot! The woodworm!'...or even a smart stuccoed Georgian town house, all cracks and creaks, stuffed with the ghosts of powdered provincials...or even a Barn Conversion, with real oak beams and the ghosts of cows...

This house was supposed to have been a *surprise* for me. He was so proud of himself for having gone out and arranged the whole thing ('Actually, I got *excellent* terms" he said smugly) including all the furniture, carpets, garden...he even went out and bought the pictures!

So what's so New Man about that...I have to make a confession to you, Journal, since you're going to be such a *private* friend I must hold nothing back. I suppose I should have mentioned that I have cancer, killer lumps, no big deal. We are, after all, quite old friends me and It. Like an old married couple who hate each other but manage to live together somehow. Understanding of foibles but hating them all.

So you see I am not allowed to seem ungrateful when Graham goes ahead and arranges our lives around me. Though I am, of course I am! But he's so like a jolly child, or a dog. Tail-wagging and so keen to please. It would be cruel and nasty to tell him what I really think.

So he has captured me, put me in this box, tied pretty ribbons around it so that I can't escape.

And if I was to complain that I'm bored to death during the day when he's managing things at Samsung (that's what he calls his job - 'Managing things') I think he'd be confused and even hurt.

He seems to imagine that a life based around the trivial exigencies of Estate life is all I'm fit for, or have the energy for...but I boil and I burst and - even after such a short time of it (and didn't blasted Tammy *predict* all this so accurately! She knows me far too well.) I'm bored to death.

Graham just treats me like a charming pet and a toy and an invalid and it's so stupid! I am *never* in the sort of pain that would stop me from doing the normal things other people do. His attitude is an insult. And I know that if I complain he'll bloody humour me. Which would make me madder ...we've never had an argument yet...(Noises. Is he getting up at last? Hold on. No, the Beauty Sleeps...)

And since he's still sleeping, and I'm still bored, I'll take you on a tour of our little Kingdom. Slippers off. We don't want to wake the Sleeping Booby.

*

We'll start with what is referred to in the Midland Dreamhomes brochure as the "Baby Bedroom". That's because, being the fourth bedroom, it's so tiny nothing but a cot and a play chest would fit in. I have claimed it as my Study. I will keep you there, Journal old thing, and I will lock the room. For your - and my! - security.

The wallpaper is a jolly pink, with flowers and fluffy bunnies in blue and mauve cavorting all over this florid field. Graham has promised to replace it with a more sedate Regency Stripe or something, "When he gets round to it". I have the feeling that Graham is probably useless at DIY - and he knows that I am, too, so I may just have to live with fluffy bunnies.

It has three items of furniture in it: a white melamine chest of drawers which is empty. I wouldn't dare stuff it with clothes or anything heavy! I bought a very similar hate-object from B&Q or some other DIY place when I was a student in Bristol. Putting it together took twice the energy that helping it fall to bits took! It kind of dissolved into a powdery mess of flaky chipboard in the third week. This didn't stop me from using it for the entire four years of my B.Ed. It always brimmed with jumpers and jeans and undies and tops. Ii became - eventually - a pile of clothes and chipboard, so that wherever I went, parts of the chest came too.

No, that aint dandruff, that's my furniture.

The second Item is my Regency sabre-leg chair, which I bought in a Bristol junk shop for three quid and tried to fix. The repaired leg looks ugly, but it keeps the chair up.

Thirdly, my thirties walnut desk. This is the only thing (apart from the chair) in this house that is truly mine. Chris and Barbara, medical friends from the old days, gave it to me when they moved to America. I love it. Its dark figured walnut is ugly as hell really. It's also far too big for this room. But I don't care. It's a finger up this house.

For the rest of the room: The curtains are all fluffy bunnies, matching the wallpaper.

There are pictures of Peter Rabbit and a happy clown.

The carpet is dusky blue with wavy lines in pink.

I suppose the room was decorated in pinks and blues so that Midland Dreamhomes plc could cover themselves - against a little boy baby or a little girl...

(Let's get out of here)

Now next-door is the room cheerfully referred to as the "Guest Bedroom" by Graham. Furniture: Two single beds lying chastely side-by-side like dead nuns. There is also a dressing-table, a chest-of drawers and a stool, all in white-stained fake (?) Ash. There are built-in white melamine-faced cupboards that are empty, and smell it.

The top of the dressing-table is empty too. So are the bedside tables, which I forgot to mention.

It's so sterile, barren,...

I think I hate this room more than I do most things. Even the way the thick bottle-green carpet tries to intimately tickle me through the soles of my slippers is intensely unnerving. Let's close *that* door!

...and the next one has the Husband asleep in it. The door is open so we can safely peer in.

This is our saccharine lovenest, frilled, laced, straight-jacketed, Graham's ideal picture of the perfect place to have sex. (He never uses the word sex. He calls it Makin' Whoopee or Soppytime or in Summer, Squelch. Sometimes he says 'Let's make love', and that's when my heart sinks because I know he's going to be so slow and *considerate*, as if he's afraid of hurting me, and it drives me crazy)

On the subject of Sex: I have so much in me, unexploded bombs. I often wonder if I love Graham. I must work that out. Hang on, let me think.

While I'm thinking. Graham matches this room perfectly. Like him, it's luxuriously padded without being *fat*. Too much body hair, unnecessary wasted stuff, quite useless for anything. And he always smells sweet, Graham. I'm sure he shits Jasmine - or Paco Rabanne, actually. He has a horror of bad smells.

The dressing-table is my favourite hate-object. It is kidney-shaped, ash stained black. It has a pink moiré fake-silk cloth over it. This is protected by a kidney-shaped piece of glass on top. All the sterile dressing-table accoutrements - the scent bottles, the Victorian pressed-glass green vanity set - everything was bought by Graham when he furnished the house. While I sat in Bristol, fuming between radiation treatments.

'See?' he said proudly when he first introduced me to this particular cell of my prison, 'you won't have to do a thing, it's all done for you.' Then he asked, pressed up against my suddenly rigid body - stifling any possibility of protest - whether I loved him.

I said that I did.

He lies there so happily inert, I have a passing desire to slip into bed next to him. Oh no but I couldn't bear the sudden grasp of arms, the enveloping stench of last night, the suffocation of his love.

Bedroom 4 is another child room, designed for the sort of twelve-year-old sexist twit who makes models of death-dealing tanks and aeroplanes, dreams of steaming battlefields, murders aliens by the million on a bleeping computer, experiments with his penis in the light of a shakily held torch.

...I won't take you on a tour of the downstairs rooms right now. I'm a teeny bit tired. I think - after I've locked you up safely in the Study - I might just creep into bed and be swallowed up.

CHAPTER TWO

Good afternoon. Guess what: I've just been allowed into Joan Belling's house! This is indeed a great honour, no-one is ever invited *there.*

She came waddling up to me in Sainsbury's this morning - I have no idea why she suddenly decided to talk to me - and started chatting away, as if we were old friends. 'Look at this', she said, showing me a carton of 'Home-made' soup, '£1.29 here, and do you know I paid £1.32 in Tesco's. Amazing.'

'Indeed,' I said, as if these things were of huge importance.

This sent her off on the subject of the differences between these superstores - prices, quality, which has the edge. 'The thing about Tesco's', she said, summing up and effectively cancelling out her whole argument, 'I know it's a little further away but you see they have these marvellous profiteroles. I'd willingly drive the extra few miles for those. Yum! Do you like profiteroles?' Joan's voice is plummy and rich, very Green Wellies.

I nodded enthusiastically. Actually, I don't.

'Still, it *is* nice to have this lovely shop so near by, it's like having this massive food-machine on one's doorstep, and no having to deal with ignorant shop assistants...' Her concentration switched to a jar of pickles, 'Bloody expensive for a mere impulse-purchase, what?'

I warmed to her. I liked her saying 'bloody' and I liked the easy way she'd slipped into conversation and her total lack of pretension.

'Joan,' I felt suddenly emboldened to ask, 'what made *you* buy a house in Estate ville?'

She started slightly, returned the pickles to the shelf. 'Is that what you call the Estate? Estate ville??' She grinned widely and I had a glimpse of jagged, stained teeth like those of an old lioness.

I laughed. 'It's my word for - well, take the Tweeds for example - '

'Can't bear the woman', she said. 'I have to positively fight her off sometimes. She comes to the door on any sort of excuse, just like - whatsname, in the Archers?'

'I'm afraid I'm not exactly a fan - '

'Whatsname, I can't think of it. Anyway, she'd use any excuse to get into my house you know.'

'She just wants to compare!' I said.

We laughed together and suddenly we were friends, shopping together, very suburban, chatting about our lives, about food, about the Estate. Then when we finished shopping, we drove back to the Estate in convoy.

Her car, by the way, is an incredibly beaten-up old Fiat that she drives like a peasant-killer, 'That's what it's made for', she'd probably say. I believe we hit 80 on the dual carriageway. I wasn't going to let her beat me. My Fiesta may be small but it goes like the clappers, as Graham would say. I'm sure I could have overtaken her, but I resisted out of politeness.

And when we got there she asked me in for coffee and profiteroles. Out of admiration, I think, for my driving.

This definitely shows that she trusts me. Her house is a junkyard, a jumble of mess and madness, the sort of place from which an archaeologist in a thousand years' time could reconstruct the entire history of the last half of the twentieth century.

There are cardboard boxes full of books, sewing kits, photographs, dead Christmas presents, stationery - I don't know what else, I couldn't root through more than one while she was in the kitchen.

There are magazines all over the place - mostly old Vanity Fairs, Country Lifes, that sort of thing. There was even a copy of Hello! under a mound of debris. The Shropshire Star lies open on what may be a Regency sofa table, displaying the Weekend TV Guide. There is an ashtray full of cigarette butts, a mail-order catalogue, a glasses-case, a notepad covered in tiny writing I didn't have time to read, a cardboard box which claims to contain Monopoly - it is sellotaped shut, may never have been opened.

And that's just the sofa-table! The rest of the room is just more of the same.

Beneath this junk and largely hidden by it is, I suspect, some superb furniture. What looks like a seventeenth-century linen chest sits smothered by magazines under the window. An oak (?) gate leg dining-table beneath more detritus, one leaf folded down against an opposite wall. Country shieldback chairs in need of repair stand awkwardly about.

There is some evidence of a recent attempt at hoovering the stained Chinese rug, which is probably one of those chintzy affairs with flowers and scrolls but it died so long ago it's hard to tell.

'Yes I know,' Joan said, coming into the room with a trayload of mugs of coffee and a plate of sticky lardy-cake, 'it's all rather a mess I suppose.' Then 'Sorry, no profiteroles,' she added, to my relief.

'Oh, it doesn't matter - ' I started to say, then realising that what I had just said could be misinterpreted, I tried to cover up - ' What I mean is - well, I suppose it is, really,' I surrendered with a self-effacing laugh.

'I know it's bad, dear. I'm perfectly aware of my failings.' She sat next to me on the creaky Biedermeier sofa, swept some paper off the table and plonked the tray on top of what remained. 'I regard housework as pandering to the trivial, don't you?'

My daily routine played itself in my head. Get up make coffee for self and husband eat muesli with him bid him good-bye ablute and then, hoover and dust, hoover and dust. 'I have to pander to the trivial. There's no choice,' I said sadly.

'Oh dear,' she said, 'that sounds suspiciously like a Cry from the Heart. You must be bored rigid. Have your coffee.'

'I am, I am! You should see my house. It's like a picture in a brochure by one of those security companies who run private prisons! It's as full of clichés as a dolls' house. It's - '

'Dear dear dear,' she clucked.

I'm afraid I indulged myself, then, in the sad old Housewife's Lament, too long and old to repeat here. Everything just spilled. And when at last I ran out, paused for breath, I dared to check for her reactions and there was nothing but a broad grin on her face. 'But how - I mean, how do *you* survive? I mean, you're not the sort of person one expects to find on the Estate. I would imagine you living in a half-timbered tiny cottage in a minuscule village happily pottering about the place and writing histories of the local church - that sort of thing.'

'Oh, I've done that!' she said almost contemptuously. There's no mileage in that. No no, my dear, places like this are *filled* with Mystery. Charged with drama. Full of Real life.'

'Really?' I said, laughing, 'Where?'

'I can't tell you yet. Not yet. I have to trust you *completely* first. I have to know that you're the type who doesn't blab. *Then* I'll tell you.'

This is creepy, I thought. Just then, Joan sounded like one of those paranoids stuffed with peculiar obsessions. 'Well, I'm good at secrets,' I said, hoping she wouldn't tell me anything mad.

'I think that's probably true but don't rush me. Let me get to know you first.' She drained her coffee and lit a cigarette. 'Have you finished dear?'

Expecting to be offered another coffee I nodded that I had.

'Well run along then!' she said, as if addressing a small child. 'Off you go.'

Off I went.

*

I suspect she *is* mad. A disappointment. I would have said neurotic not insane, but now I'm not so sure.

CHAPTER THREE

I've made another friend. At least I think so.

This morning I was sitting in the garden reading my Guardian (getting hold of a copy of the Guardian is impossible round here. The Poman has offered to keep one for me, but I hate committing myself to anything, it's strange, that, but if I were to accept his offer, I'd feel guilty if for any reason I missed a day. I don't want to be beholden. Or something. Is this strange? Perhaps the real reason is that I'm beginning to detest the man. He always makes a snide comment when I buy the old Grauniad. Anyway, the end result has been that for the last couple of days, rather than go into his den, I travel miles from newsagent to newsagent on a Guardian search. 'Not much call for that round 'ere Missus' sort of thing) when this child leapt over the garden fence. This was a creature spattered with mud, who landed badly on the rockery and straightened with a loud cry of 'Shit!'

I was startled. Dropped the paper. Saw the intruder. 'You boy!' I said absurdly, like some character in a William book, 'Come here!'

'Oh excuse me' the child said and I realised that beneath the muck my unexpected visitor was a girl, 'I didn't know there'd be anyone here.'

'What's that got to do with it?' I asked. 'The point is, you're on my property. Who are you?'

'Look madam,' the girl said, approaching warily, 'I didn't mean to trespass, really, it's just I was looking for somewhere to hide out for a while. I'm in flight, you understand.'

Then I registered that there was blood welling from her calf. 'You're bleeding,' I observed.

'Oh I *am* sorry', the girl said, having obviously recovered her poise, 'Not only do I invade your privacy but I drip blood over your lawn!' She glared at me and I felt as if I had just offended Boudicca mid-battle.

I laughed. 'I don't think the blood will affect the lawn much,' I said, 'though it could upset your parents.'

'Bugger my so-called parents' she said casually, pulling a cast-iron chair under her and sitting down.

I studied my uninvited guest with a feeling of amused respect. My five years as a teacher has taught me not to show surprise at anything a child does. Though I must admit that the easy way with which this child used swearwords jolted me just a tiny bit.

Description: She looks around twelve or thirteen, tousled short-cut brown hair - very tomboyish. Her face has the charming ugliness of the cartoon gargoyle, something to do with the sharp green eyes and high cheekbones. The chin is what ruins any possibility of this ugly duckling ever turning into a swan - it juts out aggressively, and has a crust of picked acne just at the tip. She wore cut-down blue jeans - too large, and a red plaid shirt.

'Well make yourself at home,' I said.

'I have.' She dismissed the irony in my voice. So what are you doing here?'

'That was what I asked you,' I said, trying not to revert to Teacher Tone.

'I was just looking for somewhere to hide out, somewhere I can slip off to if needs must. You don't mind do you?'

'Oh no, not at all. I don't mind.'

'You're all right,' she said suddenly as if she'd just made up her mind. 'You're normal.'

'Well thank you,' I said, actually quite flattered. 'So how about letting me wash that cut of yours?'

'Jean says you're strange, that I'm to keep away. That's why I came.'

'Oh I'm strange alright. Who is this Jean?'

'That's the one calls herself my mother. Only she isn't - ' the child stopped herself, as if afraid of giving something away.

'I see,' I said. Then 'Tell me, what's your name?' I wanted to know which of my neighbours had described me as 'strange'

'I'm called Annie Tweed by them,' she answered reluctantly. Then, as if seized by a horrible thought, she looked at her watch. 'Good heavens,' she said melodramatically, in an assumed upper-class drawl, 'is that the time? They'll be looking for me for dinner. I must fly!' And without another word she left, leaped over the fence and was gone.

I do miss the children sometimes. Just now and then...I never should have given up the job! Though I must admit it was getting more than stressful...perhaps I *will* look in the Times Ed...that'll upset Graham...well, some time.

*

Radiation and tests day. Not too horrid, just undignified. I was home by four.

Jean Tweed was waiting for me by the front door. 'Ah Mrs Alpert' she said, the way a parson greets a parishioner. 'So glad you're home.'

'Mrs - uh Tweed?' I shook her limp, ringed hand. 'What can I do for you?'

'Would you mind if I came in? I need to talk to you.'

I have decided not to like this woman. I felt deep resentment at her inviting herself into my home. Nevertheless I had no choice so I unlocked and ushered her in.

'Gosh,' she said, in a stagy paroxysm of delight, 'it's simply lovely. Do you mind - ?' She toured everything in the room as if shopping in Santa's grotto. 'But this must have been the Showhouse, surely? Everything so lovely, so *perfect*!'

I had no idea what she was talking about. 'Showhouse?' I repeated stupidly.

'Oh you know, they sell them with everything. And what *taste* they have!'

'They?'

'Who would have *thought* of combining this delicate salmon carpet with these green drapes! Perfection.'

'Drapes?' I began to suspect that I was being subtly insulted, but hadn't quite worked out how.

I realise now, of course! The bitch was implying that neither I nor my husband could possibly have any taste, so we ordered the house ready-made!

'Curtains dear, they call them drapes in the States. Oh dear, I'd nearly forgotten why I came to see you in the first place.'

'Would you like a cup of tea or something?' I offered reluctantly.

'Frankly Mrs Alpert I'd much prefer the Something, but I don't really have the time. No no, let's just sit down and have a little talk shall we?'

'Please,' I said, indicating the sofa.

'It's heavenly' she said, sinking into the sofa and running her hands over the fabric. 'So soft, so tasteful.' She sighed, and deep disappointment with life in general sighed with her.

I sat opposite on the newsmelling matching armchair and fiddled with a ceramic bowl on the sofa-table. 'You were going to say - ' I prompted.

'I believe you met our daughter Annie yesterday,' she began tentatively.

'Yes I did. She cut herself on the rockery.'

'Not your fault, not your fault at all my dear, ' Jean Tweed waved the injury aside. 'We're so used to it I'm afraid. She's always coming home with scrapes and bruises. Two months ago she broke her arm. She's supposed to be in school, of course, but there's nothing we can do to get her to stay there once we've dropped her off. She's through a window and away before the teacher can say Jack Robinson. We're trying to get her into a Special School at the moment, though that's so expensive - '

I could have said, why, that's my area of expertise, I know all about children, and so on, suggested the right people to deal with the child - all that - but I didn't. I suppose I don't really want to get involved with this woman. Though I rather like the child...I'll have to think about it.

Instead I said, 'I'm sorry to hear that.'

'Ever since the accident when she was a child - oh dear I'm so sorry, I don't mean to ramble on and on like this, it's so boring for other people. All I'm saying is she's a rather - *disturbed* child, and you must certainly never take her seriously. And do tell me if she bothers you, I will try to keep her away.'

'Don't worry Mrs Tweed. I quite enjoyed your daughter's visit.'

'*Did* you?' Her flow stopped for a second. I couldn't read the expression on her face at all...but on reflection, I think it was fear. Just a little flash of fear.

*

Graham sprawled flopped-out on the sofa, some of his attention on the nine o-clock news. I stirred my decaf.

'That Tweed woman from next-door came in today,' I said casually, inserting words between my husband and the television. Usually a difficult process.

'Hunh?'

'The woman Tweed. The one Joan Bellings calls Mrs Snobby.'

'I see yes very nice.'

'Yes isn't it?' I said, sipping. 'She admired the house tremendously.'

'Very nice.' Graham allowed the suspicion of a smug smile to sit briefly on his face.

'Yes. Absolutely enthused about everything.'

'Good good,' Graham mumbled, wishing I would shut up.

I added more sugar to the coffee and stirred loudly, making tiny pinpoints of coffee-splash on the polished surface of the sofa-table. 'She admired your taste.'

'*Our* taste dear' my husband murmuringly corrected me.

'No, dear. Your taste...anyway, she thinks you were terribly clever for having green "drapes" with a salmon carpet.'

Graham must have sensed the edge in my voice. He gave me some attention. 'Well, I was told that it's fashionable. So I chose it. Don't you like it? You have to say if you don't like it.'

'No, it's not that,' I said, feeling as if I was perhaps delving a little too deeply.

'Well, what is it then? Isn't my lovey-honey happy with what Big Bear did for her? I'll change it immediately. Come here.' He extended his bear arms with a bear smile.

There's nothing that grates me more than Graham in Fluffy-Bunny mode! 'No no please don't. It's fine!' and then I knocked the cup of coffee over, brown splotch on the salmon carpet providing the perfect excuse for escape...

*

Seven weeks married and my husband doesn't understand me! This is corny, this is awful. (I have just pushed his cloying arms off me and slipped into my study, because I can't sleep and my mind is churning all over the place.) I really don't know why I accepted his bloody proposal. We were perfectly happy with our Arrangement, as I used to call it. He'd come over once or twice a week, spend the night, he was easy and considerate and I quite liked it. It took the whole sex-thing off my mind because I do need it, and a convenient regular man does save one a tremendous amount of energy looking for it. And when I was younger I certainly wasted a great deal of time looking for it!

He had just sorted out the traditional Messy Divorce.

I had just learned that I have Hodgkin's' Disease and was feeling rather frightened and vulnerable.

And my relationship with Barry (steamy stormy and sickening) had finally ended with a crunch.

So when Graham said that he'd been offered this job in the Midlands, why don't we marry and just drop all this burden of Past and piss off, I said 'Yes, alright then' like the girl in the Philadelphia commercial and we laughed and that was it.

Trapped, boxed, chained.

And that was when he came up here and bought a Showhouse and lied to me about it.

Seven weeks into our marriage and he's already lying to me! WHY do some men assume that women are there to be lied to?

MANY men.

Weak little chickens, must be protected from the world, lies are easiest.

I don't really hate him for this. He just assumed that I would like everything in the Showhouse, so he bought it. Ready-to-wear. All he wanted, I suppose, was that I should admire him for his taste, be grateful to him for having done everything, be happy.

I had better go back to him, slip into that stiflingly hot space, try to sleep...

CHAPTER FOUR

Yesterday was a particularly lovely, clear, crisp early Spring day, quite unnaturally warm, too. The daffs are well out now, and the lawn is starting to look less like an inept hair transplant.

I was waiting for a chicken to cook, flopped out on a lounger wishing the sun was hot enough for me to get a tan, languorously scanning the Sunday Independent, while Graham was new-mannishly chopping vegetables in the kitchen.

Well, when I say I was reading the paper, let's be honest, my mind was on less wholesome things. Like Tom Meld next-door who had removed his shirt to drag a clackety lawnmower over their weeds. I know he's no good looker, this Tom, but at least he's slim. Wiry, muscles sticking out of his pinked flesh. And I was wishing that I had a muscly, young, *different* man.

It was a sort of 'ifonly' thing, not serious, after all I'm still attractive, even at thirty-five. I'm slimmer than I used to be, I look quite good nude. Oh, not quite a *firm* as once, but still the right shape.

I have always thought of myself as slightly - good old word - plain. At school, and even after that, at the Poly - I always had stunning-looking girlfriends. They were all men-magnets, jolly come-and-go girls. I was the one who'd get the *sincere* men, the save-the-world men. And, of course, the *married* men.

Which is exactly why and how I got landed with Graham, I suppose.

He certainly seemed a good idea at the time...my years of passion with Barry - passion on my part, convenience on his - had led to nothing like the permanence he always promised. (Strange how - because I couldn't have him, perhaps - I actually wanted to spend my life with that man.) The bastard will never leave his wife. He's far too weak. I believe - even now - that Barry really genuinely loved me. That's the reason he was so angry with me so much of the time. He resented me for having allowed/made him love me. And the threat to his cosy home and family.

I met Graham through Barry.

They were good friends. Graham was such a *trusted* friend Barry let him meet me. And when I was really vulnerable one night - old tale, don't want to write about it - Graham took me to bed...Trusty old Graham!

I have long suspected that Barry introduced me to Graham in the hope that G would free him from me. Paranoia? It could have been subconscious, of course. MAYbe.

I wonder if they ever discussed it, the way men do, 'Do feel free to take her, good fellow, it won't be for long and you'd be doing me a tremendous favour...'

No no no! None of that!

I was telling you about yesterday afternoon, wasn't I?

I was startled out of my reverie by a 'Psst!'

The Psst was coming from the back fence, from the Lake Walk. I dropped the newspaper on the table and ambled to the fence. I was expecting the psster to be the girl from next-door on another Mission.

It was Joan, half-crouched behind the ill-grown hedge. 'Quick! Over here!' she whispered urgently.

I peered through the picket fence and struggling privet. 'Hello Joan. Going for a walk?' I asked. 'It's a fine morning. Why don't you come in?'

'Don't be silly dear, there's no time for tea. Where's the husband?'

'Uh - inside. Chopping vegetables.'

'Good. Pretend you're looking over the fence. Enjoying the view.'

Bemused, I pretended to enjoy the 'Lake' - a muddy pool of water which lay dead over what had been a slagheap, the surrounding concrete path, the sickly trees which leaned desperately away from the stagnant water. 'Why?' I asked.

'Never mind why. She's visited, hasn't she?'

It sounded a little like an accusation. 'She? You mean Jean Tweed?'

'Yes her. What did she have to say?'

I realised that it would be a good idea to humour her. 'Well, she was talking about her daughter - the funny one, looks a bit like a garden gnome - '

'Yes yes, the one they call Annie. And - ?'

'That's right. She tried to tell me, I suppose, that the girl is quite mad and I'm not to believe a thing she says.'

'It's disgusting!' Joan ejaculated, as if her worst suspicions were confirmed.

'Those weren't the actual words,' I said in mitigation.

'You had better come with me.' Joan said grimly. 'Come on, you can climb over the fence easily enough.'

I wasn't too keen on this undignified operation. 'What about Graham?' I asked, 'I can't - '

'There are far more important things going on here than your blasted Sunday Roast, girl. Come on, lift yer leg!'

I couldn't refuse, could I? She's born to command, I thought, hitching myself carefully over the fence. I wonder if that means I'm born to follow, I thought with a sigh, remembering all the times I've trailed after people in the pursuit of things I considered unnecessary or dangerous.

'Now keep low,' she whispered hoarsely 'and follow.'

We slunk like guerrillas along the fence for a few yards, until we were at the back of the Tweed house. 'Very quiet now,' she whispered.

We waited in silence for about a minute. The Tweed's garden was deserted. Birds sang throatily, unconcerned and dispassionate.

'Morning Joan gel!' The hearty voice made me jump.

Harry Frost stood on the path grinning down at us, a ragged terrier at his heels.

'Good heavens Harry you made me jump,' Joan complained.

'Sorry and that,' he said with a bemused grin. 'On Obbo, are we? Nice morning for it!'

The Major was dressed in ill-fitting blue jeans and a cowboyish plaid shirt, sleeves rolled up over white-haired forearms. His absurd moustache was sprinkled with a decaying portion of his breakfast.

'Exactly. And we'd appreciate it if you'd buzz off a bit before you ruin everything. There's a good fellow.'

'That's a bit radical,' Harry said, obviously offended. 'I want to play too! I've had a great deal of experience in these matters. Did a lot of slinking about in Burma. Jungle warfare stuff.'

'Oh don't give me all that!' Joan said with a sniff, 'You drove trucks and ordered men about at Aldershot.'

'That as well, madam, that as well. I promise to be good - ' He dropped to his haunches beside us and the dog did a round-robin of face licking.

'We would be better on our own,' Joan grumbled, although she had evidently accepted defeat.

'I'll be quiet as a moose.'

'A moose?' I said, beginning to grin. I like the man. He's clearly quite as mad as Joan, though in a different way.

'Morning Mrs - uh. Didn't see you down there. Nice day, eh?'

'Very nice,' I said dryly.

'Hush you two!' Joan commanded. 'Something's happening.'

Something was indeed happening in the Tweed house. There was the sound of a door slamming, and Jean and Allen Tweed emerged onto the patio.

'It looks as if Spring has finally sprung,' we heard Jean say. 'Of course it's too early to really tell. Last time I decided that the frosts were over we lost half the garden.'

Her husband muttered something inaudible.

'Get the chairs out dear will you? We can have lunch alfresco.'

He replied half inaudibly, though I caught the words 'ozone layer' and 'skin cancer'. She interrupted with a sharp 'Get a move on dear, don't argue.'

'Down!' the Major commanded suddenly, as, with an arm around our shoulders, he forced us onto our knees. Privet pricked my cheek.

Whistling laconically, Jean Tweed was making her way down the gnome-strewn path to the fence. 'Morning,' she said casually, peering over the fence at the absurd trio, 'Nice day!'

'I swear,' said Joan with dignity as she struggled to stand up against the still-restraining arm of the Major, 'if I hear that phrase once more I shall spit!'

'Well it is, isn't it?' the Tweed chirped.

I could have exploded with embarrassment. The Major, on the other hand, had determined only to give name, rank and serial number.

Joan was quite unruffled. 'Very well, I accept your remark,' she said, as if making a reluctant concession.

'Looking for mushrooms?' Jean Tweed asked sardonically, 'Quite the wrong time of year you know.'

Joan gave a mannered, casual laugh. 'Really,' she said.

There was the sound of cast-iron being scraped across patio. 'Well, you'd better hide again. Here comes the Slug.' She turned and strolled away toward the house, where her husband was extracting heavy chairs and tables, as if the encounter had been a perfectly ordinary and matter-of fact occurrence.

'All right, ' said Joan, 'get down!'

'What?' I whispered, 'I think I'd better get home...'

'Don't think!' the countrywoman whispered hoarsely, 'Just listen!'

'She's right you know,' Harry said, 'Gel knows best.'

'I'm getting heartily sick of all this!' Allen Tweed's voice floated over the fence. How much longer? I feel like a prisoner in Colditz. Never knowing when the war will end. All my escape attempts fruitless. I tell you - '

'Yes dear. Bono.'

'What?'

'You heard me. Isn't it a lovely day?'

'Yes dear, it's a lovely day. But don't you understand? This is *exactly* what I mean!'

'Aren't the flowers lovely. Look at the dear daffodils coming up. And the crocuses. And listen to the birds singing away. Aren't we lucky?'

'Lucky.' he echoed.

'Lovely house, lovely family. Really, we have everything we could ever want in life.'

'Everything' he echoed again.

Allen Tweed and I were obviously soulmates. But why? WHY was I being forced to listen to the private (and, I have to add, deeply boring) conversation between our neighbours? I began to feel that unless I extricated myself from this knot of spies, I would become truly claustrophobic. So when I heard Graham's voice calling my name from our garden, I shook myself loose and, muttering, 'I have to go', I crawled off toward my own house.

'She leaves just as it's getting interesting' I heard Joan mutter as I climbed over my own home fence.

*

'Oh there you are,' Graham said cheerily as I entered the garden in my undignified fashion. 'We'll have a gate put in for you dear, if you want to walk along the lake...come,' he said, beckoning conspiratorially, 'we have a guest.'

'Guest? Who? Where?'

'In the sitting room,' he said, and winked.

And there she was, sitting prettily on our sofa, in a pink, flouncy party-dress. There was a smear of lipstick on her mouth. 'Annie? Good morning,' I said.

The contrast between this picture-book child and my visitor of yesterday was almost incredible and I had to say something. 'Are you off somewhere special?' I asked smiling with what I hoped wasn't amusement, 'Aren't you looking smart!'

'You're talking to me as if I was a child!', the child complained.

'I'm sorry,' I said and sat in an armchair. 'Well! How about a cold drink of some sort?' Then I added mischievously, 'or would you like something stronger?'

Annoyance flashed briefly across the girl's face. She didn't like being made fun of. 'No, not at present,' she said, keeping her composure. 'I came to talk.'

'Well,' said Graham, leaning against the door jamb, 'Is this women's talk or am I allowed to listen?'

'What do you think?' Annie turned to me for an opinion.

'No no,' I said, 'it's up to you.'

'I don't mind, as long as we can trust him', she answered, as if Graham wasn't in the room.

'Oh absolutely!' Graham spoke with indulgent good humour, and just for a moment, you know, I had a pang of doubt. I can't explain it.

'All right then, listen.' The little girl spoke low, with an intensity I have never seen before in seven years of teaching. 'I suppose I am going to tell you the whole story.

'My name isn't Annie, to start. It's Mary Dyne Fortesque.

ANNIE'S TALE

'I was born into a lovely family, eighteen years ago. Oh don't look so shocked, I know I'm small for my age! But small as I am, I have the heart of a young woman.

'My parents were wonderful people. Father did something or other in the City and my mother had fabulous bridge parties all the time. We were the toast of Hampshire. Balls, coming-out parties, we had everything. Father was terribly rich, you know. Rich as Croesus. We had a Rolls Royce. Grey with a number plate that said RIC 1 H. Because Father's name was Richard and he wanted everybody to know how rich he was.

'Anyway, when I was fifteen, both of them were killed when the Rolls, driven by our drunkard chauffeur Alex, went out of control and fell off one of the Chilterns!' She paused to check our reactions. I placed a look of horror and concern on my face.

'It was terrible for me' she sighed sadly. 'I'll never forget the day when Alex came into the house, covered in grease and grime, the steering-wheel of the Roller still clutched in his bleeding hands, to give us the awful news...' the child wiped a tear away with an impatient sleeve.

'Terrible for you,' Graham said. His mouth was pulled down in a parody of sympathy and there was a twinkle in his eye.

'Yes it was,' she continued. 'Anyway, my brother Charles and I were left alone for a while after the funeral, until one day *they* came.'

'They?' I asked stupidly.

'Yes! The ones who call themselves my mother and father. Mr and Mrs Tweed. *He's* my uncle, my father's brother. *She's* his whore!'

'Well!' I said, about to reprimand her for the word.

'Does that shock you?' she asked, her eyes now full of tears. 'That's exactly what she is. He pays her to pretend she's his wife. She's just one of those women of the night, contracted. You see, it says in Father's will that his brother

Allen was to look after us if anything happened to them. But only if he's married, and settled down. And nobody would ever marry him!' she said contemptuously, 'He's such an arsehole! Oh I'm sorry to swear but that's what he is. An incompetent, a man who's failed at everything he ever tried. Do you know, once he was offered a partnership in Virgin Airways, right when it was starting. By Ricky Branston himself. And he refused. Fifty quid was just too much of a risk for him. What a worm!'

We shook our heads over what a worm Allen Tweed is.

'God knows where he found that woman. My detective says she was a Lady of the Night. An upper-class whore. The sort who sleeps with all the members of parliament, all the Lords and things. And now she's my pretend mother! Oh doesn't it *sicken* you?'

Graham and I looked suitably sickened.

'I shouldn't be surprised if they weren't planning to kill me for my money, or rather, mother and father's money. The generous allowance they've been given to look after us isn't enough for them...' she was weeping again and I handed her a paper napkin.

'One thing puzzles me,' I asked gently, 'what happened to your brother? What was his name?'

'Oh, Peveril,' she said with a snuffle, 'I have no idea! He said he would run off to America, if he ever got a chance...but maybe they got to him first! Probably dead and thrown away into the Thames...There's only one thing to do,' she announced, 'I'm going to run away.'

This last phrase was said so melodramatically, with such actorish resonance, that I knew the exact territory we were in: Barbara Cartland meets Jean Plaidy.

I must have shown a trace of disbelief then, because the child suddenly stared searchingly into my eyes and said, urgently, 'You look as if you don't believe me.'

'No no,' I said reassuringly, 'I was just smiling to myself.'

'Don't say you don't believe me, ' the girl pleaded, 'please don't say that!' Her eyes brimmed, overran. 'I've been praying and praying that I'd find somebody to believe me. I need your help. Please...please...'

Her sobs were wracking and consuming, as if she was being washed away by unstoppable waves of long held-in grief. I can't explain how *real* her misery was. And I couldn't help it, I melted. Don't blame me! I know the whole story is ridiculous, obviously the product of a lonely child with a massive imagination (and too much Mills & Boon!) but at that moment all my cynicism evaporated and I hugged her, comforted her. It felt as if this child had longed for a mother's affection...and I so needed to give my love to a child. Gates opened... (I have never admitted, in written or spoken words that I might want a child, or children. Never! Though some would say that my decision to become a teacher was a way of dealing with this. It makes me too vulnerable! In the early stages of my relationship with Barry, when he was promising happy-ever-after, I assumed we would eventually end up together and there would simply *be* two or three children...they would be part of the scenery. But if I mentioned this to Barry he'd go hard and quiet. I suppose now that he was so screwed up by his own miserable childhood that he hated the idea of inflicting the horrible experience of growing up on anybody else.

(He hated his father. He was the only child in a grim booklined house, where ideas were far more important than emotions, and the Boy was treated as an unnecessary appendage. An expensive and importunate and bothersome idiot. I'm rambling. And thinking, Barry could never accept the idea of me and children because it would be Commitment.

(I need to ramble some more. When it became obvious that there was no future for Barry and me I did wish - oh, very secretly - that I had a child...and that was about when my Lymphoma was diagnosed...)

I do like brackets. Parenthesis. Life should have far more brackets. (By the way...)

It was peculiar, that diagnosis, the first invasion of the Body Snatcher, the Stranger. I had gone to the GP because Barry persuaded me that the swelling of the gland on the left side of my jaw had lasted too long. There was never any pain, just a sort of discomfort like knowing that someone else was in the house, an uninvited guest...

The GP sent me to the BRI - the Royal Infirmary. I was now officially *infirm*! They confirmed. I had some radiation treatment, very clinical, quite painless. The swelling went down. Everybody was happy. It all seemed perfectly mechanical to me, very unthreatening. I went to work as usual, told nobody (except the Head; she needed to know why I needed the odd Wednesday off). The Medics assured me that 90% of patients are easily cured. And I thought I had been. Until a year ago, when the lymph-gland on the right side of my throat swelled up.

Graham knew about my illness when he asked me to marry him. I remember saying, 'Well you can forget children. If you have any hopes of founding a dynasty you'd better find someone else!' What I was really saying was, I don't want to have a child and then have to leave it just as I'm beginning to enjoy being a mother. He didn't ask me to explain. He just hugged me so *warmly*, with so much love that I decided then and there to try and love him.

I never thought I'd hug a child and feel

CHAPTER FIVE

That was the doorbell. Joan. Just as I was getting into my writing, too! People conspire, I sometimes think, to forbid me any introspection. Lucky thing this time. I was about to be maudlin.

I am coming to the sad conclusion that Joan is off her head. She knows Annie's story, and she believes it! And she's so *urgent* about it. It's as if she has a Mission now. She actually believes that she has a duty to save an innocent girl from the machinations of evil greedy step-parents. And she's determined to enlist fellow-converts.

'You see! You see!' I told you there was something sinister going on. You've heard the story. You understand! She says you do.'

'She - you mean Annie - '

'No, Mary Dyne Fortesque. She must have told you that's her real name?'

'Uh, yes, ' I said, heart sinking.

'It's a terrible story, terrible. I feel deeply for her dear, deeply. I've promised to rescue her. If I don't do something she'll run away. Can you imagine? That poor little thing, all on her own...'

'She says she's eighteen. That's quite old enough - ' I said with a barely repressed smile. (I was remembering Graham's laughter, after the child left. He had found the episode hilarious, and was puzzled when I didn't join him in mirth)

'Did you hear those people, did you *hear* them?' she asked, ignoring my comment.

'You mean the parents?'

'The *step* parents,' Joan corrected me. 'She said "Bono", do you remember? When he was complaining about his lot...'

'"Bono"?'

'Obviously a code-word, Harry says. Meaning, shush, there's somebody listening. Don't you see? It proves they have something to hide...'

'But - '

'But nothing. It's the proof I need. Now I know the child is telling the truth. Oh I know she embellishes the story a little, all children do that. Didn't you say you've been a teacher? You should know that.' Joan's puffed-up frog face glistened with sweat. She spoke like the Newly Saved.

'We must plan,' she said determinedly, 'Plan. You will help her, won't you dear. Those Tweeds are bad, very bad. Between us I'm sure we can save that innocent girl.'

'Joan,' I said tentatively, 'even if what she says is true, surely the situation isn't desperate. Maybe all the child needs is love, friends, ...'

'Don't you understand yet? They're going to try to kill the child, that's certain. They want the money. Didn't she say?'

'She *implied* - ' I began to say.

'Well it's obvious.' Joan was adamant. 'You can tell what sort of people they are. They're what we call "Cwmtuither" round here. It means, "not of our flock". Ancient Celtic I suppose...'

Fearing a history lesson, I brought her back to the subject. 'Joan,' I wondered, 'If you're so sure, why don't you go to the police? They'll know what to do.'

'Bunch of flatfooted morons. They won't raise a finger until poor Mary is lying dead...poor soul. Mark my words.'

'But what - I mean, what can we do? How can we possibly protect - uh - Mary?'

'I don't quite know how to answer that question yet. I must think hard about it. For the moment we'll just have to wait and watch. Keep our eyes on them all the time. Give them no chance to do anything dastardly. And since you live next-door, you could be the saving of that child!'

'Me?'

'Just keep your eyes on them. Make friends with that Jean woman. She likes you, she approves of your curtains. The newsagent tells me. Oh I keep my ears open and my eyes peeled, you have to in this place. Go and visit her. Take her a cake or something.'

'A cake?'

'I'll knock one up for you if you're incapable.' She stood up fussily, pushing her cup of tea aside as if it was a fetter keeping her somewhere she had no time to be. 'See if you can gain her confidence. Tell her I'm as mad as a March Hare, so she won't connect you with yesterday...do it this afternoon, I'll be back with a cake in a jiffy.' And she left.

*

I stood on the doorstep of the Tweed's Cumbria, a still-warm sponge cake on a paper plate in one hand, the thing weighing me down like a plaster cast. It took courage to ring that bell. Why the hell had I let that domineering woman push me into this? I sighed deeply, a sigh which said well this is fate I must play this game because I have no escape. Tring (More like dingle, dong dong boing, dingle). Fate.

Jean Tweed opened the door distractedly, as if she was expecting me. She waved me in and I found myself in another microcosm of Spireslea life.

The carpet is purple, thick and deep, sucks at the shoes like a swamp. A chandelier drips languidly from the magnolia ceiling.

One side of the room is devoted to dining: the Regency repro table, six Sheraton-style chairs, seats upholstered in purple and green stripes, mahogany suffocated in honey-coloured lacquer. The sofa and two chairs are a blaze of bright floral, a William Morris pastiche, deep enough to swallow guests whole. The sofa-table is an oval, onyx-topped nightmare, resting on cast-brass angels.

I suppose I must have stared at all this and possibly allowed a trace of my horror to show through. Honestly, I felt as if I was in a funfair side-show! I don't think she noticed, because she said, sweetly, 'It is lovely, isn't it? I did it all myself, you know, with a little help from that wonderful shop in London, Chester and Something.'

Oh what a clever girl, I thought, unlike me, who came into my Spireslea prison all ready-made. 'Yes, it's lovely', I said insincerely.

I suddenly realised that the room had a centrepiece. Annie. Standing stock-still, hands behind her back, like a soldier standing easy. 'Good afternoon Mrs Alpert' she said, as any perfectly polite young girl would.

'Good afternoon,' I responded.

'Why don't you go upstairs and read your book dear', Jean suggested. 'She loves her reading, the little dear. A perfect little bookworm.'

'I know,' I said.

The girl stared at me, brow briefly creasing with suspicion. 'I'm reading "Little Women"', she said in a precocious little-madam voice. 'It's by Louisa May Alcott.'

'Yes well get along and read it' Jean commanded. 'Such a trial,' she sighed as the child trooped upstairs on a carpet which said 'ploof' at each step. 'Well do sit down, dear, I can see that you're burdened.'

I held out the cake numbly, started to make a casual remark, but she waved me and the cake aside. 'I didn't mean the cake, dear, I meant spiritually. Spiritually burdened. Heavy with the weight of the world. Do sit down and tell me about it.'

I sat awkwardly, the rejected cake on my lap, warm and cosy, feeling like a warm friend. (Child?)

I remembered why I had come. 'I just wanted to say how sorry I am about yesterday, ' I started.

'Sorry? Why?' She was obviously determined to make me suffer.

'Well, ' I said, disconcerted, 'I mean - '

'You mean for spying on us.' She had evidently decided to help me out. 'Don't worry dear It's what I would expect from that dim woman. Would you like a cup of tea?'

Yes I would. 'Please.'

She swept off to the kitchen, which was divided from the lounge by a low plant-covered wall. From which she continued, as she filled the kettle and laid out cups.. 'That woman Bellings has been spying on us since we arrived, you know. She's quite obviously mad, thinks we're international criminals or some such. She doesn't understand that all we are is normal people who just want a quiet life. Sugar?'

'What?'

'Do you want sugar? Only I'm not sure we have any. None of us use the stuff.'

'No thanks.'

'At first it used to annoy me terribly,' she said, returning effortlessly to the previous topic. 'I wanted to tell the police, get an injunction or something. Allen says she's harmless, he doesn't want any - fuss, you know? Publicity. Ignore her and she'll go away he says. Hmm. I think the milk is alright.' She sniffed the cream-jug appraisingly.

The cake was beginning to feel like a baby that's let go of its bowels. I leaned forward to unburden myself of it, to put it on the onyx table. It lay there sad, sodden, defeated.

The kettle boiled aggressively, clicked off.

'But she doesn't go away. Yesterday she was lurking behind the fence - oh, I'm sorry, -' she said mockingly, 'You know that of course.' She peered at me, waiting for a reaction.

'I really am sorry,' I said lamely, 'She - '

'Yes, ' she sighed, 'I can imagine...' She came into the lounge now, bearing a huge tray heavy with expensive china and exquisite biscuits. 'What did she tell you? How on earth did she convince you that my family and I are worth spying upon?' She pushed the cake aside with the tray so that it balanced precariously on the edge of the table.

I felt truly desperately ashamed. The woman was so rational, her impatience and disgust with Joan's peculiar antics so unfeigned...in contrast Joan seemed thoroughly eccentric. 'I - '

'That so-called Major is involved too, isn't he? He's as mad as a hatter. Milk?'

'Yes please.'

'It's all too much, really it is. Especially on top of all the trouble we have with Annie. And to think we came here to get away from stress!'

'Trouble?' I asked numbly, remembering my mission.

'It's what I told you about when I came to visit you. The girl is ill, dear, ill. She's a compulsive liar. Lives in a world of her own. Which would be fine if it wasn't for the fact that she involves other people in her nonsense' Her cup sat on its saucer at a dangerous angle on her lap. She became suddenly aware of the dangerous situation, and made an appropriate adjustment. I could see that her hand was shaking.

Then she said, in a shy whisper, 'I really wish we could be friends.' Her eyes stayed down in her lap, as if fearful of rejection.

The phrase took me by surprise. And for the second time this week I felt touched. It was done so sweetly, almost girlishly.

'I - I will,' I said. It didn't sound sincere - and yet I wanted to mean it.

She looked up with a forced smile. 'Well...well...' Which meant, 'We'll see.'

I tried to meet her eyes, and after a while I succeeded. We smiled at each-other. I didn't believe in either of us. Neither did she. Now I knew that all she wanted me to do was to leave. 'I'd better be going, ' I said. 'Graham will be home soon.'

'Ah, your handsome husband. Well you mustn't keep him waiting' she said cheerily.

I stood, placed my sipped-at cup on the free two inches of table. 'You'd better take that with you', she said, gesturing toward the cake, 'God knows what's in it.'

'What?'

'Well you never know with the insane dear do you.'

I picked up the sponge and bore my humiliation to the door.

'Don't let her get out of hand, that's *my* advice. Play along with her. Humour her a little. That's what one's supposed to do, you know. Good-bye dear.' Jean said, and closed the door leaving me wondering if it was Annie I was to humour, or Joan, or both.

*

Days passed and I heard nothing from either of my neighbours. My life slipped back into Bored Housewife routine. Shopping expeditions to Sainsbury's. Cleaning the house. Cooking for Graham.

It's strange how efficient I've become at Keeping House, despite the fact that I absolutely hate every moment of it. My mother, if she was still alive would never believe it. She used to be a cleaning-freak, always called me a slob when I was young. I was normal! - I mean, my bedroom was always piled high with clothes and junk and love-letters and even when she visited me in my digs in Bristol, she'd zip around the place with rags and Vim before she'd even think of sitting down and having a cup of tea.

She would never accept that I have changed since then, that I have learned the trick of switching on the automatic button and becoming a flash of lightening. Zip! Clean! Shine!...I reckon it's the fact that I hate doing it that has made me so good - so that I have developed a hundred tricks to make it go faster.

Barry taught me the trick. It's one of the very few useful things he ever gave me.

I miss my parents...I know they loved me and I tried to love them back. Well, I remember well loving my father, though he was rather grey and quiet and defenceless (or at least, he was after he retired. It was as if somebody had sneaked up behind him and clicked the off switch. Before he gave up the jungle, he had the reputation of being wild, impossible to work for, unpredictable, ruthless. I know this because I tried working for him once, during a Summer Vac. The Company, I need to say, made something impossibly technical to do with Heat Conservation. It involved fascinating silver material - fibreglass, I think - and lots of Velcro.

Anyway, you should have seen him! He'd go out onto the shop-floor when he had one of his flareups 'Oh Oh,' his secretary Judy would say, 'He's got a strop on him' and she'd head for somewhere safe as he raged, throwing fibreglass and plastic tubes into the air as if trying to shred reality so that whatever it was that annoyed him could never have happened in the first place.

A week there was all I could take. Yet, the strange thing is that, although his shopfloor workers changed often - few lasted as long as I did - the office workers stuck it. They were deeply loyal to him, though I know some called him That Loony - they knew he went crazy sometimes, but they stayed. Perhaps they knew the truth - that he was only frightened, which was what made him vicious. my theory is that he lived in perpetual fear of the world collapsing around him, like that fellow in the French comic - is it Asterix? - who is convinced that at any moment the sky will fall on his head.

Well it may be that when he retired he finally accepted that nothing more could possibly go wrong, so it was safe to switch off.

And then he became a sweetie, the kind of grey man who, in parks, will innocently entertain other peoples' children for hours.

Mother was a dragon in her way, too. She was what they call a Big woman. Or, maybe, B I I I G. She would have been called 'big-boned' by kind aunts in her youth. But she grew older, she learned to dress aggressively, so that in her brash colours and loud-shouting scarves people would notice that she was Big - but would never dare say *fat*. Another thing that amazed people was the sheer *speed* with which she moved through life. Like a lithe and nervous athlete. Which is fairly intimidating in someone of that size.

When she and father were together they looked like a couple out of a twenties film comedy - the tiny grey man and the bullying wife. But they weren't like that: they were in love all their married lives, and she used to treat him like her beloved pet - sort of like a Pekinese - pamper him, do all sorts of small love-things for him every day.

And when he had the stroke, she was panicked - that's the only word for it. As if all of a sudden something impossible had happened, no-one could understand how impossible, and there was nothing anyone could do...she kept saying 'It's unfair, it's unfair' and she went on and on saying that until Barry and I developed a theory that there had been something amazingly secret and special between them, something she would never dare to talk about. And then one day we went to see them and she was dead across his body, the two of them stretched out on the bed almost like a cross...I suppose she had gone into the bedroom, found him dead and had a heart-attack.

That's one possibility. There are others.

I've always been so jealous of my parents. Why can't I believe so much in another person that I can truly give all my love without any doubt or restraint? That's been the problem with all my relationships. I can't give me away. With Graham - hang on, telephone -

CHAPTER SIX

What a weekend... Graham decided that we should see something of the countryside, so we went to Ludlow on Sunday. Much medieval - some castle! - many ghosts...this made me think of death. I don't know what happens afterwards, and I don't really care. I mean, if the Goddists are right, then I'll find myself outside heavenly gates and I'll say, 'Gee sorry I didn't believe in you. Forgive me.' And he or she or it will let me in, because I've never willingly hurt anybody.

And if there are no heavenly gates and no god and no saints and I just blip out, then so bloody what.

I'm trying to avoid this fact: that it's quite visible now. I look in the mirror and I look lopsided, off-centre. I catch peoples' eyes sliding away from mine when I talk to them, slipping a fraction to my swollen side. Then their eyes go hooded and I get angry. I'm talking about Graham, I suppose. Why can't I just write about it all easily, like I swore I would! Because it *hurts*! Then he comes into the kitchen and insists on helping me to wash up and then he asks quietly, 'How are you today' and I want to swear at him.

Shut up. Shut up. I swore no self-pity and that's fine, as long as no-one *gives* me pity!

Graham is quite a hero, really. He puts up with it all and he must be hurting like hell. And he has no-one to talk to about it. He must have deep hidden strengths. More than I thought. I wish I could help him...

Sometimes I feel so guilty about being ill, about what it does to others. This is silly.

Change subject; it's so good being on my own! This morning I tidied and cleaned like a wild woman, as if determined to scrub every trace of life out of the house. No forensic lab could identify a single hair that is not mine, a single fingerprint.

*

I've just returned from the Post Office. I had to go to slimy Derek's because frankly my cleaning fit left me tired and for once I didn't feel like scouring the countryside for my Guardian. Incredibly, he had a single copy, yellowing already in the stand outside the shop. I considered leaving the money on the doorstep, but that seemed a little silly, so I went inside to pay.

'You've made me happy' I said cheerily, paying for the paper'

'Good,' he slimed, 'we like happy customers.' Then, as he handed me my change, 'Why?'

'At last', I said, pointing to the paper, 'you're catering for intelligent people.' I realised how arrogant I was being, so I added a self-mocking, insincere smile.

'We have the occasional member of the chattering classes in here' he said, and rose in my estimation. 'Mind you, ' he added chattily, 'You're not the only one. That Tweed woman usually buys a sheaf of qualities.'

'Oh,' I said, mildly interested, 'all of them?'

'Well it's usually the Times, Financial Times, Telegraph and Guardian. Sometimes she buys a Sun as well, especially when they have one of their particularly salacious headlines. She looks right embarrassed, that's for sure. Then she says, "I'll have some of the ridiculous with my sublime please", always the same joke. Funny bird.'

I laughed. The man is more intelligent than I thought. As there was nobody else in the shop and I felt like a rest before starting home, I asked him what he thought of them.

'Those Tweeds?' he smiled archly, 'Funny lot. That woman, now I've met her sort before, they want to be Queen of the Cul-de-sac. You know, run coffee mornings, start up embarrassing Amateur Dramatics clubs, that sort of thing. Funny thing is she does none of that.'

'Really?' I asked. I began to weary of the conversation and was looking for a way out.

'Had one of those the last place I worked, Monsham, in Kent. Fine village, rather like this one. We had a queen there all right, anybody who wasn't invited to her drinks parties just wasn't anybody. I was never invited of course.'

'Shame, ' I said with a courteous smile which I hoped he would interpret as a sneer.

'Just shows what a snob she was. Oh hello Mrs Bellings.'

'Morning Derek,' Joan said heartily as she bustled into the small shop, appearing to fill it. 'Telegraph please.'

'I was just telling Mrs - uh - about the Tweeds. Strange that they won't fulfil their proper *role* around here.'

They exchanged a look I couldn't interpret.

'Not as strange as some people would think,' Joan said. 'Oh it's all right,' she smiled, 'Sally is one of us.'

'Oh good', he said smugly. Then 'I say, isn't it time we had a talk? Wait a minute.' He let himself out of the counter, went to the front and shut and locked the door. The Open/Closed sign was twirled around with the flick of a wrist.

I felt trapped. The shop shrank around us.

'Have a look at this', Derek said as he pulled a folded A4 sheet from the inside pocket of his jacket. It was a muddy photocopy of a letter.

'Oh well done that man' Joan said approvingly as she read the letter. 'Look at this!' she commanded and I read it over her shoulder.

The letter was typed on a solicitor's letterhead, very formal and gloriously old-fashioned. The name of the firm was something like 'Greaves Twitchell Logan and Warrington' though that wasn't it. If I remember rightly, it said Dear Mrs As per your instructions we have studied the documents in question and have come to the following conclusions:

1) In the event of the death of the legatee, the Estate reverts;

2) In the event of proven insanity, or the legatee's being declared unfit by reason of sickness or other acceptable cause, the estate reverts.

We hope this answers your questions.'

' - and there we have it! The proof! You see?' She turned to me triumphantly. '*Motive!*'

'But what does it mean?' I asked, feeling as if I knew.

'It's perfectly obvious.' Joan's tone was that of a nurse describing the purpose of a potty to an idiot. 'They had asked the lawyers to check what happens when little Annie - or I should say Mary-Dyne - dies or goes mad or something. That's why they're telling everybody that the child is crazy. And if that doesn't work...' she lowered her voice theatrically, '...see what I mean?'

'Surely there could be another explanation?' I said tentatively.

'Nonsense dear!' Joan snapped, 'It just proves that the child is telling the truth.'

Do you know that feeling, when you suddenly realise that things have just left your control? It's like being on an aeroplane, as you strap yourself in.

'We are going to have to start to make serious plans now.', Derek said pompously and I looked at him with barely suppressed renewed revulsion. It was the way he said it, snivelling like Uriah Heep. Through his nose, with a sly and solemn look that was totally insincere. Like a bad actor. I noticed for the first time that he was wearing a waistcoat under his jacket, from which a watch-chain looped down dramatically. In this hot weather, too. Damp stains, yellowing, peeped out from under his arms.

'So we will, so we will,' Joan said.

'We should go to the police.' I suggested.

'Waste of time. They can't do anything, and they won't. Besides, are we going to admit to them that we have been interfering with Her Majesty's mail?'

I sighed.

'What we need,' she continued, 'is a whatyoucallit, a troop, a gang, a small lot of people who can watch over that poor girl and leap in as soon as anything happens...'

'Well well,' Derek said with exaggerated admiration for her sagacity, 'I think that's rather a good idea. People we can trust. We must recruit!'

'We had better not refer to them as a gang,' she said, 'that smacks of criminals. No no, we're the forces of *good*, that's what we are.'

'We could call ourselves FOG' I said mischievously, remembering the Forest of Acronyms in the world of education, 'you know, for Forces of Good.' I meant it as a joke.

Joan stared at me as if I had just solved the mysteries of the universe. 'That's brilliant!' she gushed, 'Wonderful! FOG. I do like that.'

Derek was thrilled, too. He looked like the Fat Boy of the scout troop, let in on the mysteries at last. 'We can have regular meetings,' he said, 'and planning sessions, and secret codes!'

'If you like,' Joan said, slightly taken aback. 'Anyway Sally here will be our linchpin, with her nose to the ground and her ear to the wall...'

'Not terribly relevant in detached houses' I said cynically.

'In a manner of *speaking* dear, in a manner of *speaking*.'

CHAPTER SEVEN

Last night Graham announced that he has to go to Japan for two weeks for what he calls 'Tlaning and Deblief'.

'When?' I asked.

'On the fourteenth. Will you be all right on your own?' he asked tentatively.

'Of course I will!' I answered, too abruptly.

You see, when I went to the hospital yesterday they confirmed my suspicion that the radiation treatment isn't working. I say confirmed, because for the last week I've had fevers on and off. Night sweats. I wake in pools of water, especially around my head. Graham can't have failed to have noticed, though he sleeps like a dead whale. He has said nothing about it, he has been waiting for me to say something. And I won't. I know he's worried and I don't want to make that worse.

I have also lost a great deal of weight. This is strange and frightening though in some ways I like my new trim figure. I was always heavy in the thigh area, now I'm almost lithe!

The thing that made me really worried was my discovery that the glands in my groin are swelling. It's only just noticeable but it's there and I can feel these new intrusions, new lumps coming to visit.

That nice Dr Jennings said 'We'll have to consider chemotherapy' and the word rang in the air, hanging over our heads.

It's a word that has always frightened me, but after the first shock of it I felt something like relief. I knew somehow that the radiation wouldn't work. And now they want to admit me...I hadn't wanted to tell Graham, I had been putting it off, I was about to say something when he made his announcement, and now maybe I don't have to. If I can arrange to be in hospital when he's away...why not? It's ten days until he leaves, that could be just about right. The Doc tells me that my chances of survival are pretty high anyway. Apparently, I am now on what is called the B Stage of the disease. 65 to 75% of patients in this stage are cured by chemotherapy. That's a high success rate. I suppose.

Come to think of it they told me that 95% of patients are cured by the radiation treatment and it hasn't worked on me. So I will have to think very carefully about this. I'll call Dr Jennings in a minute, discuss timing with her.

I must admit that the idea of chemotherapy doesn't appeal. Dr J warns of nausea and hair loss. It's not that so much, it's the loss of dignity...I must make the call.

*

Joan has decided to set up what she calls a 'Hide' in my garden. This morning (I am writing this late afternoon, waiting for Graham to get home) she and Harry arrived with great panels of tongue-and-groove pine and boxes of windows and armfuls of tools. 'We'll build a Wendy-house', Joan explained. 'It's brilliant, isn't it dear. Harry's idea. A Wendy-House right on the fence, and we can take turns sitting in it, observing the doings next-door. Look!' She ripped a large, bulky brown-paper wrapped parcel apart. 'One-way glass. See! We'll make the windows just there. It'll be lovely...'

'A Wendy-House...' I said, dismay creeping into my voice.

'Don't you worry Mrs!' Harry said, 'It'll be the envy of the neighbourhood. See here!' He pointed to pots of green varnish in the back of his Volvo estate. 'It'll be dapper as a racehorse. Smart as a pin!'

I felt the cloying arms of Spireslea crushing me. A Wendy-House! A further blot on my landscape and I didn't have the heart or soul to deflate the enthusiasm of this mad pair. And say 'Look, I could never have anything so desperately corny littering my garden, just so that you can use it to fulfil your silly paranoid fantasies. Take it all away and burn it.' Why didn't I say that? WHY?

Instead I spent the rest of the morning helping them dig out the plot and pour in ready mixed concrete for the foundations. The work was very hard, very physical and it angered me that I should have to do it, so I didn't feel guilty when eventually I just sat down on the lawn, pleading exhaustion.

I have to admit, though, that building things is peculiarly satisfying. Tomorrow we'll start putting the floor down if it doesn't rain. *If* the concrete has hardened. *If* I can't think of an excuse for not having that monstrosity in my garden...What the hell. It's in keeping with the general monstrosity of the house.

I know exactly what Graham will say when he gets home. Or if not say, think. He'll be delighted. He'll be so pleased I have a project to spend energy on. He'll love the fact that I am doing this project with my neighbours - 'friends' - and he'll adore the end result. A man who buys a Show House in Spireslea could only approve...

I don't feel like writing any more now. I'm going out into the garden to have a look at the sodden grey rectangle of concrete.

Jean Tweed was hanging over the fence when I got outside, staring at the pile of parts. 'What on earth is it going to be?' she asked without preliminaries. 'Pardon me for being curious,' she added.

'A Wendy-House' I said airily.

'Good lord,' she said, trying to work out how to react. 'Well that'll be nice. Like a little guardhouse, I suppose?' she said.

'A guardhouse?'

'Well I presume, since I see the mad Belling and Frost duo are helping you, that they have some dire plan for this thing. I saw them motoring off when I arrived.'

'They're being very kind', I said, resenting her perspicacity.

'Oh are they.' Her tone was flat. She seemed tired. She looked into my eyes with a puzzled frown.

I felt appropriate shame. 'Look,' I said, 'You said you want me to - well - humour them. That's what I'm doing.'

'All the better to spy upon us I expect!' She sighed. 'This is all beginning to get just a little bit on my nerves.'

'Well what do you expect me to do?' I asked, exasperated and wishing this was all happening to other people.

'All we want is to be able to live a quiet life. It's that child, that - oh it's not as if I don't love her, of course I do. But everywhere we go, there's trouble. Do you know, when we lived in Luton it was the same. Did I tell you what she did?'

'No,' I said.

'She used to terrorise the neighbours there. That was why we moved out. You see, she decided that she didn't like these people, the Johnsons, something to do with them being snobby to her. So she used to hang about their house making faces through the windows. Oh you're lucky, dead lucky she has decided to like you. But the last straw came when she took their two cats and fed them some meat doped with my sleeping pills. Then she sellotaped their tails together and put them back in the garden. When they woke up there was a dickens of a row, spitting and howling and fighting...I love cats you know. So did the Johnsons...'

'That's terrible,' I said.

'Oh, she has done worse things. Once, years back she decided that she wanted revenge on a doctor for having given her an injection. She hates injections. Well, she pretended to be terribly ill - she's a great actress you know - she had put chalk on her face and made herself vomit all morning with some sort of emetic - we thought she had swallowed poison you see - well the Doctor came, parked outside, and went up to her room. She asked us, in her most quivering voice, to wait outside she wanted to see the Doctor alone, so we closed the door...then there were the most horrible screams from inside the room. Horrible. We rushed inside to find the Doctor looking as if he was covered in blood, standing at the side of the bed with a look of - how can I describe it? - terror, absolute fear I suppose - on his face...holding a dead snake about two foot long in one hand, dripping with that red stuff...urgh! She can be evil. I hate to say this about my own daughter. Evil!'

'But - I don't understand - ' I said, not having quite grasped the story.

Apparently she had discovered that Dr Prewitt had a morbid fear of snakes so she got a dead one from somewhere...it was only a grass snake, quite small. And when the Doctor asked her where it hurt, she pointed to her mouth. Her asked her to open wide and she shook her head, then when he went closer out shoots the snake in gobbets of stage blood...she couldn't have had the thing down her throat, I suppose it just looked that way...'

'That's incredible....' I said.

'It is! It is! She's lying! She's lying!' I looked up and I saw Annie leaning out of an upstairs window. Her face was streaked with tears. She had heard every word.

'Go back inside! Shut the window!' Joan commanded.

'I won't! I won't!' The child screamed. She was hysterical with fury. 'She's lying Mrs Alpert! I swear she's lying! No-one believes me. No one!'

Then she climbed out on the ledge. 'I can't stand it! Say you believe me Mrs Alpert! Say you believe me!' She had gone way past any hope of reasoning with her and I was utterly stunned, I just stared, God forgive me, why didn't I just say - before I heard Annie and Jean Tweed screaming together as the child hung in the air for a moment, arms and legs flailing, before her small body thumped into the flower bed.

*

I'm to blame. Though Jean Tweed tells me she blames herself. Oh the child will recover, there's no doubt about that. She has merely broken a leg and bruised herself. The flower bed is soft, luckily. So she'll live...but I don't know if she'll ever forgive me. All I had to say was "Yes I believe you and it wouldn't have happened...

Anyway, of course the screams and the ambulance brought Joan and Harry scuttling over, filled with enough indignation to have destroyed Jean. Their faces! I couldn't bear their interrogations, or Jean's absolutely genuine distress...so I went home and ignored the door-bell (which Joan rang for a good quarter of an hour) and waited miserably for Graham to get home.

I am still waiting for Graham to get home. Typing this has stabilised me a little at least. I have stopped shaking.

I am to blame. If only I had told Joan and Harry to bugger off in the first place...what the hell am I on about, all this wasn't their fault!

What if they're right! Wouldn't it be absolutely *horrible* if the child's story is true? I mean it would explain Annie's absolute despair, her desperation....

And on the other hand! The Tweed woman's distress when Annie fell seemed absolutely genuine, I'm sure of that! Aren't I?...oh hell here's Graham.

*

The Wendy-house is almost finished and I'm glad we're building it now. After all, *if* there is anything funny going on in that house, and *if* there's a chance the child will suffer...could I ever survive the guilt if I did nothing?

The events of the past few days have made me come to a decision. I realise that like it or not I'm now involved and I have to know the truth. No-one will make up my mind for me. I am going to observe and think and watch and see. I now have a few weeks breather, while Annie is in hospital, and by the time she comes out - and I come out (I don't know which will happen first) - I'll know which side of the fence to fall.

Another peculiar thing happened today, which may or may not be relevant. Allen Tweed is unemployed! Well no big deal you may say but you see, every day he gets into his Sierra at around eight in the morning and drives off. Strangely enough I've never thought to ask what he does for a living; I just took it for granted that he does something boring and technical in the New Town - something to do with computers or engineering. He looks like the sort of man who would be a Sales manager for, say, a company that makes stainless steel exhausts. The sort of job one would hate to come across at a party.

This morning Harry came late - we'd expected him at nine, Joan and I; we needed his carpentry expertise. O dear I'm jumbling this all up. I'll start again, putting the morning into chronological order.

Eight-thirty: Graham goes off to work with an injunction 'not to work too hard' which annoys me. This is a bad start to the day.

Nine, Joan arrives with three two-litre cans of pink emulsion. I refuse them politely, pointing out that if the outside of the Wendy-house is to be stained bottle green, a pink interior would be too much candyfloss. She is offended but shrugs saying 'I had these cans lying about in the garage and I just thought...but if you don't like the colour dear...'

I make her a cup of tea and we await Harry, whose job this morning is to make the window frames. Neither Joan nor I know how to do the joints involved, which makes me more annoyed and uneasy. There's nothing we can do until he arrives.

It started to seem like one of those days that set the teeth on edge and make me growlsome and edgy.

Joan and I sit on the patio drinking tea. We watch as Allen Tweed gets into his company car, all suited and tied, and drives off. Joan clucks and grumbles.

Anyway, Harry arrived (my tenses are getting mixed up) gone ten, all panting and sparking with excitement. 'I say I say,' he puffed, 'wait till I tell you. Is there one for me?'

I poured tepid tea into his proffered cup.

'What's happening old boy? You look like you've just see a bull give birth!' Joan haw-hawed.

'Listen to this!' Harry slurped tea noisily. 'That Tweed fellow, we were right you know. Definitely rum.'

'What on earth are you talking about? What rum?' Joan snapped impatiently.

'Bumped into the Meld woman this morning while out with the canine. She's not as daft as we think you know. No, quite amusing. Well, we're sitting on the bench by the lake - she'd had some sort of bust-up with her slob again, went to the lake to have a little weep I suppose - brute of a fellow, that husband, I'd love to take a swipe at him - '

'For heaven's sake Harry, what did she say?'

'Getting to that, getting to that. Well, conversation gets around to the Tweeds you see, can't quite remember why - and she said that every morning when the Allen chap gets into his car, know where he goes?'

'Where?' I chipped in, trying to hurry him along.

'To the pub, that's where. Pops off to Little Lemmings, Dog and Duck to be precise. Sits there all day getting sozzled apparently. Can you beat that?'

'Good Lord! How does she know?' Joan asked, agog.

'Her blob Tom goes all over the country, doing something connected with gymnasiums - or is it gymnasia? - believe it or not. He saw him in Little Lemmings. More than twice, I shouldn't be surprised. He's half-seas over most of the time. Brute of fellow.'

Joan slapped her hand with a fist. 'Well! How do you like *that*!' She beamed at me, as if her whole theory had been proved by this.

'I don't quite see - ' I said, knowing that I was being provocative.

'It shows - at the very least! - that they're not what they seem! That's for sure.' She added triumphantly.

'I don't know, ' I said, 'It may merely be that the woman is such a whacking snob, she has to keep up appearances whatever. She'd hate the whole estate to know that Allen has lost his job.'

'Don't be ridiculous dear. It proves there's a woodworm in the woodwork. And where there's one - '

A window of the Tweed house banged open noisily. Our heads jerked up in perfect unison.

'Think she heard us?' Joan whispered behind her hand.

'Well we were talking rather loudly,' I said, feeling flushed with annoyance and embarrassment.

'Don't worry about it,' Harry said. 'If she heard, well that's hard cheese, now she knows that the charade is over. Bad luck!'

'That's so insensitive!' I protested.

'Stay calm,' Joan said like a nanny gathering her charges on the deck of the Titanic. 'Let's go inside shall we. Come on now.'

We allowed ourselves to be ushered into the lounge where we stared at each-other wordlessly for a minute or two. I didn't want to say anything, because I feared that if I did, I'd erupt.

'I think we should go over to my house,' Harry said eventually. 'Crack a bottle of wine. Make us all feel better.'

'Oh Harry, ' Joan said with a sigh of relief, 'What a good idea.' She linked her arm with his. 'Come on dear, let's go.' she enjoined.

I wasn't feeling co-operative. 'I think I'll stay here a while,' I said. 'I have plenty to do. I could sew the curtains. Couldn't I.'

'All right dear', Joan said sweetly. 'We won't stay there long. Little planning meeting. We'll debrief you completely this afternoon..'

And they left. I shouldn't be surprised if they skipped down the path.

CHAPTER EIGHT

The 'phone rang shortly after I had fixed myself a lunch of cold ham and salad. It was Joan. 'Hello Sally, won't you come over? Harry's place. We've gathered a few people, just our people you know. More Foggies. We're growing apace. Ten minutes?'

I gobbled down the meal and full of resentment, I made my way to Harry's Blandford.

The Third Class house. Indistinguishable from the Cumbria and the Portnoy, except that everything is on a smaller scale, pinched and squeezed into mediocrity.

Harry's house has scraggly yellow roses outside the front door, and a bell-push with a sign saying 'Pull me'.

I pulled, and to my horror the doorbell played rule Britannia.

The door opened while the tune was only half played. 'Come in gal, come in,' Harry said impatiently, as if annoyed that I had taken too long to arrive.

His tiny living-room was jammed with people. Slimy Derek was there, as was Joan, sharing a yellow dralon sofa with Margaret Meld. The woman looked awkward and insecure. There were three others standing about with cups of tea or glasses of beer. They all looked vaguely familiar.

'Sally this is May McCarthy, I'm sure you've met, she has the Portnoy at number three.' Joan said, indicating a very large woman filling an armchair.

I nodded politely.

'And this is George and Tom from number ten. You know, the one with the larch.'

The man who shook my hand was stunningly handsome. He was of Asian origin, tall, gorgeous slicked-back black hair and magnificent eyes, stunningly blue.

'So glad,' he said, 'to meet an original member.'

'Member?' I echoed.

'Of the Foggies he means dear. We're all Foggies here. Did I tell you Sally dreamed up the name?' Joan chirped.

I couldn't take my eyes off the man. I wanted him to touch me again.

'Very clever. Very good. Don't you think, Tom?' He turned to the other man who is about thirty, I suppose, handsome in a gone-to-seed male model sort of way. Blond, too well coiffeured.

Oh no, I thought, they're gay...then I thought, why should I be disappointed? What difference does it make to me?

But it does make a difference! I want George to touch me again...

'Something to drink, Sally? Beer? Tea?' Harry asked, intruding himself between me and the couple.

'No, nothing thanks' I said.

'Well then, let's call the meeting to order shall we?' Harry pointed to some dining chairs he'd provided and we sat in an awkward circle. I placed myself next to George. Tom sat on the other side of me. Harry led the meeting from the security of a frilled armchair. 'I propose,' he said, 'to conduct this meeting according to the Rules of Order. Those in favour say "aye".'

Sheepish mutters of 'Aye'.

'Good good. Any objections to my taking the Chair?' he asked.

'No.'

'It's your chair,' George said under his breath.

I giggled. He has a sense of humour.

'Excuse me Harry, ' Joan interposed

'Do you want to make a point of order?' Harry asked, with a barely perceptible wink.

'Sorry Harry. Point of Order Mr Chairman. We don't have an agenda. '

'Well does it really matter old gel? After all we all know what we're here to talk about.' he said, slightly impatient to get on.

'She's right you know.' the woman McCarthy spoke up in a broad Midlands accent. 'We should do things the way we do at school. An agenda, that's the thing. And we'll need a secretary, somebody to write down what is said. I could do that you know. I take all the minutes at work.'

Another teacher. Please everybody don't tell her I was a teacher. I'd hate her to feel any kind of fellowship with me!

I'm definitely not going to like her. It's not just that she is enormously fat and dressed in florals. She's just so pompously full of her own obesity, incapable of seeing through it.

Harry was obviously rattled but he rallied bravely. 'Any objections?' he asked formally.

We all shook our heads obediently. 'Carried then.' he said and standing fussily, he went to a battered Regency repro desk, rooted through a drawer and produced a notebook and pen, which he handed to the woman.

She paged through the book, looking for a blank page, licked her pencil, cleared her throat and said, 'Right then, let's get on with it.'

'Good, now that's all right - ' Harry sat in his place. 'I should like this to be a planning meeting, as I said. I call on Miss Joan Bellings to address us.'

Joan was unprepared for this. 'Oh well, if you wish. Should I stand up?'

'Whatever you like.'

Joan dithered for a second, then decided that standing up would involve particular groups of muscles that preferred to stay where they were. So she spoke from her seat.

'We all know basically why we're here. Here in our very estate, amongst these smart new houses, there exists a thorn in our side. Oh dear, that sounds rather stupid. What I mean to say is, there's mischief afoot and the forces of law and order seem powerless to prevent it. So it all devolves on us, respectable citizens, the forces of good. We few who - ' she realised that she had begun to declaim and stopped herself self-consciously.

'It's just like it was in nineteen forty is what you're trying to say isn't it.' Harry prompted.

'Well we're not actually facing *Nazis* dear, ' Joan said. 'Just a particularly nasty pair of greedy child-killers - '

'*Child killers*?' Margaret Meld said with horror. 'What do you mean child killers? If they go near mine I can tell you - '

'Calm down woman!' Joan commanded. 'They haven't actually killed anyone yet . Not yet...' she added archly.

'Will you tell me who we are referring to?' McCarthy insisted. 'I can't write it down unless you give me names...'

'Perhaps she shouldn't write it down.' Harry said on a sudden notion.

'Oh - ' Joan said, 'I see what you mean. Just write "T"', she said and added for our edification, 'for "Tweed", dear.' She paused so that the information could sink in. 'The Tweed woman,' she continued, 'and her drunken husband are plotting to kill an innocent little girl, and only we can stop it!' Joan had caused exactly the reaction in her audience that she craved. Faces froze in amazement and horror. 'And what's more,' she added, 'we have the proof!' Joan fumbled in her bag for a moment and then whipped out a photocopy of the lawyer's letter. She waved it in our faces for a minute, and then formally handed it to McCarthy, as if giving exhibit one to a court official. 'Read that, pass it on. Thanks to Derek here, we intercepted this letter and it proves that there is a motive.' She sat back with smug satisfaction, waiting for our reactions.

'This is from a what they call Solicitor,' McCarthy announced. 'So what does it mean?'

'To give you the background at this stage, I would like to hand over to my friend Sally Alpert here' Joan said graciously.

'Oh no, not me please,' I protested. 'You explain.'

'Oh very well,' Joan said. She had wanted a break from the spotlight. And she told them Annie's story in a far less embellished, much more credible version than that I had heard from the girl herself. In fact the story, combined with the letter, sounds utterly reasonable.

'We can forget the police,' she said in conclusion. 'They wouldn't want to know, not without absolutely concrete evidence that a crime has been committed. In fact they wouldn't raise a finger to help unless the girl is actually attacked. Dreadful. So it's up to us, d'you see?' She swept her eyes around the room, meeting those of each one of us in turn.

'I thought this meeting was, like, a sort of neighbourhood Watch kind of thing.' McCarthy said with a hint of protest in her voice. 'I never thought it was, well, *serious*.'

'It's a lot more serious than Neighbourhood Watch!' Harry said with a grim smile.

'I fail to see what we can actually, practically *do* about all this,' George said, and I felt a warm gratitude for his statement.

'That's exactly what we're here to discuss,' Harry said.

Raised voices clashed. 'Order order!' May McCarthy said. Then added, contritely, 'You're supposed to have said that Major. I'm sorry.'

'Yes, address the Chair, that's the way.' Harry said.

'Why can't we get a social worker or something,' Tom asked. 'As for me, I think it's silly to get involved. After all, who are we to interfere?'

Derek gave a patronising nasal answer. 'There's no point contacting them. The child has not been *abused*, as far as we know.'

'"As far as we know", yes! But we don't know enough, that's the whole problem!' Joan said.

I decided to make a contribution. 'I live next door to the family, as you all know. I was there when she jumped out of a window - '

The audience gasped. I had not meant to make such an impact and I continued, as if what I had just said was incidental. 'The mother Jean was very upset. I really don't think there's any abuse going on.'

'The *stepmother* you mean, dear,' Joan corrected me.

'She jumped out of a window?' George asked.

'She was upset that no-one would believe her story,' Joan said.

'You see?' Derek smiled smugly. 'You can't say there's no need for us to act.'

'Mr Chairman,' George said, 'I would like to ask a question.' Harry nodded his permission. 'It would seem that the three of you have known about this for quite a while. I mean Mrs Bellings, the Major and Sally here.' He smiled at me. 'Now what I want to know is, what have you been doing all this time? What actions have you taken?'

Joan responded a little huffily, as if the man's question had been intended to insult us for inaction. 'The child told me her story some three weeks ago and I must admit that at first I wasn't convinced. Oh I know that the latest fashion in therapy is that one should always believe the child but I know from years of experience that children are perfectly capable of lying.' (I wonder what she meant. Has Joan ever conceived? What) 'I discussed it all with Harry and he immediately understood the situation and suggested that I talk to young Sally, as she is so conveniently located. It came as a pleasant surprise to me to find out that the child had already decided that Sally was to be trusted and had told her everything. We decided to keep an eye on the next-door doings, and then when Derek discovered this letter - and the child attempted suicide - ' she waved the letter in the air, 'It was confirmed, wasn't it!'

'I see,' George said.

'And as to what we are doing about it, we have called this meeting after all. Harry and I chose you all very carefully as people we think we can trust. And here is what else we've been doing: we are presently building an observation post in Sally's garden...'

'Good heavens, it's like spies! Isn't it a little *obvious*?' Tom asked.

'Oh it's disguised of course,' Harry said.

'As a wendy-house. That's what it will look like from the outside. Inside it's going to be very high-tech,' Joan explained. 'One way glass, so that we can see into the garden. Harry will be getting brochures on all sorts of advanced surveillance equipment, that sort of thing.'

'Long range mikes, hidden cameras, all the latest trickery,' Harry added with a smile.

But to what end? It all seems a little - *melodramatic* to me,' Tom said sceptically.

'Don't you understand?' Joan was becoming impatient with the man. 'If we keep our eyes and ears open, if we know everything that goes on in that house, we may well be able to forestall a murder attempt! We could listen in on all their plotting, record what they say. That'll be evidence the police can't *fail* to accept! For heaven's sake! Surely it's worth the trouble to save a young girl's life?'

We all sat silently, as if ashamed. Joan regained her breath.

'Well I think - Mr Chairman, - I think it's a very good idea and I for one vote my wholehearted support!' McCarthy said.

'Me too!' Margaret Meld piped up, 'Well,' she said abashed, realising that the whole room's eyes were turned on her, 'I vote as well.'

'Well said that woman!' Joan approved.

'It sounds to me, Mr Chairman,' Tom said, 'that you three have everything under control.' He leaned back in his chair as if relieved that nothing further would be required of him. 'You don't need us.'

'Oh on the contrary old chap,' Harry said, 'Time may well come when we need every single able-bodied man - uh, and woman, of course, sorry, - in the Estate. Eh? Besides, there's the...uh...'

Joan rolled her eyes. 'Money,' she said, 'Money. Harry and I have already put three hundred pounds of our own savings into all this. Material for the wendy-house isn't cheap, I'm afraid. And all the surveillance equipment won't be cheap either. D'you see?'

I hadn't even thought about that! Neither Joan nor Harry had ever mentioned money to me. They must have paid out a great deal. I feel extremely ashamed.

Tom the cynic went 'Aha' at this stage, by the way, as if suspicions were being confirmed.

This caused George to reprimand him in a very wifely tone. 'Don't be like that, Tom, ' he said, 'Can't you see these people are sincere? You wouldn't know sincerity if it hit you in your smug face!'

'Don't start that again, especially not in public.' Tom warned quietly.

'You can count on me,' Mrs Meld said bravely, 'I don't want child murders around here. I'm not rich but I'll do what I can.'

'Thank you my dear,' Joan said, and she seemed to be moved.

'Yes it's all very well *some* complaining,' McCarthy said, putting down her notebook. 'I've got something put away. I can think of nothing better to spend it on, than protecting a child. Those people, ' she pointed to me, Frost and Bellings with her pencil, 'they've put their own money on the line to save the little girl. I should think we'd be ashamed of ourselves for the rest of our *lives* if we did nothing.'

'And you can count on Tom and I as well, ' George said, with a warning look at his partner.

'Sally?' Joan turned to me then. 'Your contribution has been huge already, but can we call on you for money if needs be?'

Heart sinking, I nodded. Money! Where on earth am I to get my hands on money?

'Derek?' Joan addressed the newsagent.

'Well I suppose I can afford to make a small contribution.' His eyes had narrowed, making him more ferret-like. 'I don't have much you know, being self-employed and that. But I suppose it's worth it.'

'Good oh.' Harry said. 'So what Joan and I will do is get some of those catalogues, select what we're going to need, that sort of thing, add it all up and come to see you. We have a few weeks at least, with the child in hospital. All agree?'

We nodded or muttered 'Aye'.

'Carried unanimously,' McCarthy said, scribbling in her book. 'AOB?'

'What?' Harry looked puzzled.

'AOB. It means Any Other Business.' She said.

'I knew that, I knew that, ' Harry snapped tartly. Then he covered his irritation with a forced smile. 'Any other business?'

'Not for now,' Joan said, obviously wanting the meeting to end.

'Next meeting?' McCarthy was determined to stick to the form.

'Yes, that's a good idea. Next Tuesday afternoon? That's a week away, gives us time to make arrangements and so on, eh. Everyone agree?'

Everyone agreed, though not without the odd demurral and diary consultation. Next week it is to be.

BOOK II

CHAPTER ONE

'We'll want to admit you as soon as possible Sally.' Dr Jennings said this morning. 'Really, I would hate to put it off.'

'I *have* to wait until Graham's gone. He'll be away for two weeks. That's just the right amount of time...'

She looked puzzled. 'He doesn't know we're admitting you? Really Sally, that's a trifle - '

'Irresponsible? Oh Cathy, I hate worrying him. I told you his last wife died of cancer, didn't I. '

'I know that. But don't you see - '

'He's so protective as it is. He smothers me sometimes. Besides, if I told him, he'd cancel the trip and that'd do him no good at all at work...'

'I would have thought that Japanese employers would be very understanding about this sort of thing.'

I sighed. 'I don't know about that. I just don't want him here! I don't want him to see me all...please understand, Cathy. Just support me in this.' I pleaded.

'Well the customer always knows best' she said, defeated. 'Very well, just tell me what date suits you.'

'He's off on the fourteenth. The next day would be perfect.'

She turned to her computer and tapped something out. Consulted the screen. Hummed. 'We can do that, surprisingly enough. I'll make the arrangements.'

I thanked her. I really like Cathy Jennings, she's the sort of person I'd like to have a social life with. Warm, clever, compassionate...must make things very difficult in her job.

*

On my way out I decided to be very brave and pop in on Annie in the children's' ward. And there she was, propped up on pillows, leg suspended in a cast. 'Sally!' she yelled, as soon as I came in sight. 'What are *you* doing here?'

For just a second, I felt awkward and unwelcome. 'Seeing you,' I said, with a nervous smile.

'Gosh,' she said. 'Well take a seat!'

'How are you feeling?' I asked, adopting standard hospital visitor mode.

'Tired, bored,' the girl sighed exaggeratedly. 'Depressed.' She indicated a pile of romance novels on her bedside table. 'Thank heaven for my *friends*...'

I took the reproach in the spirit. 'I'm sorry I haven't been to see you before,' I said. 'So much happening.' I added lamely.

'Oh Sally,' she said, tears springing to her eyes, 'I thought that *you* at least...'

I took her hand and squeezed it. I'm such a sucker for tears. 'I know dear, I know.' I felt suffused with guilt.

'I mean you have no idea what it's like having to live with *them*...and by now you must have realised that I told you the truth! you saw...'

'Yes dear I saw,' I said reassuringly.

'She's completely evil, that Tweed woman. Completely.'

'I know, ' I said, 'but you're not to worry.'

'Why? Why shouldn't I worry? I'll be dead soon. Dead and gone. That's when I'll stop worrying...it's so awful! Never knowing what they're going to do next...they'll do anything, anything to get their hands on my fortune, mine and Peveril's. At least he's out of it...' She sobbed pitifully. 'He's probably working as a cabin boy on a ship, I expect he's worked his way up to captain by now. He's very clever you see, miles cleverer than me...oh why don't I just run away too? I'm so frightened Sally, I'm so very frightened...'

She sobbed and sobbed, dissolved into tears and I hugged her, her wet tears damping my blouse. 'You mustn't worry my dear, you really mustn't. You have friends here on the Estate, did you know that?'

She looked up, into my eyes. 'Friends? You and Joan are my only friends.'

'No no, don't think that. Your circle of friends expands every day. That Major fellow, he's on your side and he's quite an organiser.'

'Really?' She wiped tears away with an impatient sleeve. 'What has he organised?'

'More friends,' I said evasively, not knowing how much to tell her. 'He's recruiting people on the Estate. Told them your story...'

'You're pulling my leg...' realising that she had made an inadvertent pun she smiled broadly. 'You'd better not! It'll come right off!'

I laughed. 'There, you see? You're laughing.'

'So I am. Really Sally, you're the *bestest* friend!' She hugged me again.

'I'm so glad to hear it,' I said, giving her a light kiss on the brow.

'Tell me about my other friends. Who are they?'

'Well...' I said, and gave her thumbnail sketches of the others at the meeting. She adored the descriptions, lapped up the details.

'Thank you, thank you!' she said when all her questions had been answered. 'Now it's time for you to go. The one they call my "mother" will be here any minute. She brings me fruit every day, keeping up appearances. I throw it all away when she goes of course.'

'Naturally,' I said.

'And you will come and see me again, won't you? Come every day. It's *so* lovely to see your smiling face. And you can tell me all the news. What they're all doing for me. Oh it's so *exciting*!'

'I'm glad you see it that way,' I kissed her lightly again and stood up to leave.

The child grasped my hand and pulled me close to her. 'And never forget,' she whispered hoarsely, suddenly deadly serious again, 'you witnessed it. You saw her trying to kill me.'

'What?' I said. The question shook me. Annie's fall from the window hadn't seemed remotely like a murder attempt.

'Don't forget. Whatever happens!'

'Hello dear, I've brought you some fruit.' It was the Tweed, who greeted me with feigned surprise. 'Mrs Alpert. How kind of you to come and see my daughter. ' She was holding a huge basket of fruit wrapped up in Clingfilm. She was dressed in a razor-sharp grey tweed suit. Her smile was thin, impossible to read.

'Good morning Mrs Tweed,' I said formally. 'I was just passing.'

'Yes and she's leaving now,' the girl said, and it sounded as if she was accusing Tweed of driving me off.

'Yes,' I said, embarrassed. 'Good-bye.'

'See you soon.' The child flashed me a broad, toothy smile as I left.

*

So what am I to make of that! I veer crazily from belief to disbelief. Perhaps the truth lies in the middle?...

Can't think about it now. Graham and I have just had an argument. Can you believe it? And just because I brought up the subject of the money, of course.

At first he was quite pleased to see the wendy-house going up in the garden, so I don't know why he's suddenly so difficult.

'I'm happy to see you putting your energies into a project of some sort. It's good for you to have a hobby. But a *thousand pounds*! Surely that's a great deal of money for a simple garden shed!'

'It's not a shed,' I said huffily, 'it's a wendy-house. They are a lot more expensive than sheds. There's much more *to* them...'

The actual bill for the wendy-house won't come to more than three hundred, according to Harry. It's the other stuff that's going to be so expensive, but I can't tell Graham about this. He's far too sceptical, I'd have to tell him about the Foggies, and he'll laugh. Then he'd say 'Let me sort this whole thing out' in his arrogant, patronising male way. Joan suggested a thousand as an appropriate contribution. I didn't think Graham would demur, I so seldom ask him for anything.

Anyway it opened a can of worms.

'What are you going to have in there?' he asked sarcastically, 'Gold lamé curtains? Hot and cold running water? A Jacuzzi? A few fancy *antiques*?'

Graham hates old things, as do many of my neighbours. He's the sort of person who would dump hundred year-old Windsor chairs, dismissing them contemptuously as *awweld* which, in Spires-speak means out of fashion.

'It's just... *necessary*,' I said, not feeling that there was any need to explain any further.

'That desk of yours reminds me of my grandmother,' he said, off on a tangent. (I realise that my lovely thirties desk represents my past in Graham's mind, and he wants me divorced from that so that I can be his exclusive property. Is this true? Must think about it.). 'Her house was full of rubbish like that. Her and grandfather bought everything brand-new when they moved into their house in 1926. Very fashionable at the time I grant you, but look at the stuff now! Wouldn't give it house room.'

'Do you have any idea how much good Deco pieces sell for nowadays?' I asked. 'I suppose you threw all their stuff away when they died?'

'Naturally. Skipped it. Burnt it, I can't remember exactly. Anyway if that desk of yours is so valuable why don't you sell it and get the money that way? If you can find anyone fool enough to buy it, that is.'

The thought of selling this desk makes me go cold. I really resent this suggestion of his. 'I think that's so *horrible*,' I said, really upset. 'It's the only thing in this dreadful house that's *mine*. You only want me to sell it so that everything in this house belongs to you, right? Even Me!' And then, to save me from blowing up and destroying the whole marriage then and there, I stormed out, did all the statutory door-slamming, went up to my study where I'm writing this with still-shaking hands. At my desk. The walnut veneer of which is cracking and peeling. Some of the drawer-handles are broken. The beading is bubbling off. It's as if the thing is drying out and decomposing...

I know exactly how my poor desk feels.

...it's such a nuisance! It's not like him to be damned mean. And I do want to pay my share of the Fighting Fund. After all, I'm getting a free wendy-house out of all this...horrible thing...

Graham and I haven't had a real row for ages. We used to argue quite a lot, especially about politics. Basically he's a raving Tory. During the last election I became convinced that the reinstatement of a Tory government - albeit under that nice Mr Trainspotter Major instead of the steel Tartar bitch - would end in tears for everybody. Graham insisted that he would vote Tory, whatever I said. 'I refuse to pay a thousand pounds more a year in tax, and that's that!' And I'd say that he wouldn't, that the NHS and Education desperately need more money, that the streets are crowded with homeless, that industry is in tatters because of their crazy policies...till the *cows* came home, and all he'd say was 'None of this affects me. We have private health, no children, and I don't see why I should have to pay more tax so that scroungers can have an easy life. I need all my money, especially to keep you in the style to which you are rapidly becoming accustomed...'

I was made angry enough by all this to leave the house one time. But he came after me, soothed me with lying words, said maybe I had a point, it was just his nature to play devil's advocate...then on election day he came home with a smug and secret smile and when I asked him, full of trepidation, what he'd voted and he replied

'Conservative of course' and boy was I *furious*! So disgusted I wouldn't let him make love to me for a week.

After that there was an unspoken agreement between us never to discuss politics again, though I can't allow an opportunity for the odd barbed remark to pass *entirely* by. Usually prompted by some depressing article in the Guardian...

Did I mention that Graham reads the Sun! And/or the Daily Star. Really! Don't you find that strange for a man in his position? I think he buys them because he knows it annoys me. He actually leaves them on the kitchen table when he goes to work. I shiver with revulsion when I bin them.

There are so many differences between us. Well, what do we have in common? Why the hell did I agree to marry him? What am I doing here? Oh bugger he's coming upstairs...knocking at the door - just a minute.

...well, he has agreed to give me the money, which is good. I've sent him downstairs to make a cup of tea, and later I suppose I'll have to make love with him in payment.

God he's a boring lover! Or rather, predictable. I must admit to enjoying our jousts sometimes, at least. I mean, knowing everything that's going to happen has its advantages. After all, one knows just how long it will last, for example; that when I roll over afterwards with the obligatory sigh of deep satisfaction, that the red eye of the digital radio-alarm will wink '23.25' exactly...

*

The doorbell rang at ten this morning. Joan, come to work, with George attached to her like a grinning limpet. She was carrying curtains. He had a box of tools and that crooked, wicked, brash, little-boyish smile. It's madly attractive.

'George is going to be our joiner,' Joan informed me breezily. 'Harry has had to go to Northampton for something-or-other, luckily it turns out George is a whiz at this sort of thing.'

'It's a hobby of mine,' he explained, 'I like doing things about the house as they say, repairing antiques and so on.'

'What do you think?' Joan unrolled the ready-made curtains which were regency striped in blue, green and pink. 'Marvellous sale at Rackhams, you should look in.'

'I'll get to work shall I?' George said, grinning again damn him. I couldn't get my eyes off him. It's not just the grin...he wore a t-shirt, really tight, his arms bulging aggressively out of the short sleeves. It was a shade of turquoise, and it glowed like neon in contrast with his skin. And I could see his nipples straining at the cloth...I deny it's lust. I mean it's true his smile should be banned for the protection of the innocent - it's just that he exudes warmth, and I *want* some of that.

I was thinking, I know he's gay, that nothing I could ever do would bring him near enough for me to *bathe* in him... then I thought, stow it, it's wasted. I'm acting like a teenager lusting for some two dimensional pop idol.

I carried the tray of tea and lardy-cake out to the wendy-house, determined not to even look at the man. I had decided to appreciate him purely, aesthetically. To congratulate God for having had such good taste and having employed such delicate artistry. I would be polite and charming and make him want me as a friend...it was the only way to get near him, to wallow in his being near.

I placed the tray on the repro Victorian cast-iron table at which Joan sat in a cast-iron chair, picking at the hem of a curtain. 'Pity about the sun,' she said, 'I had hoped it would at least make an appearance.'

'Yes,' I said politely, 'so had I. Though a little rain would also be nice.'

'I'm afraid we shall have neither.' Joan waved the sugar-bowl away. 'If I take these up say eight inches, they'll be perfect.'

'Good,' I said. Then I raised my voice, called 'George! There's tea out here!'

'Won't be a minute.' His voice, amplified by the dark mouth of the wendy-house door, was happy and preoccupied.

He emerged a few seconds later, preceded by the Grin. He was holding his left forearm with his right hand.

'What's the matter?' Joan asked, 'hurt yourself?'

'I'm afraid I have,' he said, removing the hand and showing quite a lot of blood.

'Let me look!' I said, leaping up with far too much alacrity.

'Rather silly really,' he said, 'I tried to cut a piece of wood in the window, should have taken it out and done it on the bench really. Very stupid. That's what happens to the lazy carpenter.'

'Better come in and I'll wash that for you.' When I said this I was painfully aware that this scene had been played out in so many movies. And written millions of times in bodice-rippers. 'And as she laved warm water over the wound, their eyes met...and slowly their faces drew closer, closer and then they kissed, as if all their lives had been preparing them for this moment...'

My heart was beating like a little girl's as I led him to the kitchen, telling myself each step of the way, this is far too corny! I must steel myself. I'm a married woman! Oh God, cornier and cornier! And anyway! He's NOT available NOT available!

Besides, Joan was there tagging along as a - let's face it - welcome chaperone, following us to the bathroom like a jolly sheep dog.

'No dramatics now,' she said heartily, 'I've done quite a bit of nursing in my time. In the war - '

George sat on the toilet seat cover (salmon pink) so that I could wash the blood off his forearm in the wash basin. The water turned rust.

'Nothing but a scratch,' Joan announced triumphantly in her I Told You So voice. 'What a lot of fuss.'

I managed to avoid glaring at her.

'You'd better take your shirt off young man or you'll look like a massacre victim.' She chirped. I dabbed the wound dry and stepped back so that he could obey her order.

He slipped the t-shirt over his head and I could swear that Joan knew that my eyes were no longer under my control.

George has a perfect body. Wide shoulders, strong chest with a tuft of shiny black hair in the cleft. Mound of abdominals, like hills with a deep dark central valley at the lower end of which, just above his belt, is a deep tangled knot of hair in which the invisible belly-button nestles...

I tore my eyes away, picked a tube of Germolene out of the medicine cabinet and, shaking, handed it to him. 'Here,' I said, 'rub this on.'

He took the tube from me and looked straight into my eyes. Again that grin, that damned senseless grin, splashed across his face. He knows?.

'Thank you', he said.

*

So the script wasn't acted out according to appropriate Hollywood tradition. And it couldn't have been. Even if Joan had not been there, even if George hadn't been homosexual, it wouldn't have happened. You see, when I saw him trying to rub Germolene onto the scratches - with blood trickling out, getting in the way, staining the fingers and streaking the cream so that it reminded me of my toothpaste, I thought about AIDS and had a sudden rush of fear. I had already touched his blood, it had washed over me. Homosexual or heterosexual, by the way, I would have had the same thought. Do I have any open cuts?...Quick check.

Thinking about it now, how stupid! I have my own hungry invader, my creeping death.

Anyway, the whole idea of the fulfilment of fantasy No 32b went sour on me at that moment. And as soon as George and Joan went back to work I washed and washed.

CHAPTER TWO

Graham came home ultra-randy last night. This was not welcome. I had spent a great deal of time washing up after our lunch, tidying, sorting things out. Also, I had some pain and had to take one of those blasted painkillers that make me feel woozy and unsteady. Interestingly, they seem to bring on a headache - transfer the pain from one part of the body to another. I need to ask Dr J about headaches. Note. And also these deep pains at the base of my spine.

I was standing at the kitchen sink when Graham let himself in at about 8.00. He entered silently, crept up behind me and startled me with a sudden embrace.

Fantasy No 21c: A beautiful Beverly Hills condo. Afternoon. Wife stands in kitchen in frilly nothings, sensuously laving dishes clean. He enters. (Cross between Tom Cruise and Roger Moore) Sneaks up behind her and surrounds her in hairy arms. She turns, slowly, showing her face filled with expectancy and longing and kittenish lust. He: 'At last my darling! How I love you!' She: 'I know...'

Reality No 21: Wife standing in kitchen confused as to whether to wipe over the cooker or go and lie down. She has a headache, and her old dressing-gown hangs on her like the visible proof of just how she's feeling. Husband enters silently, tiptoes up to her and grabs her like a rapist, burying her in the folds of his stomach. Wife receives tremendous shock, turns to fight the intruder off, realises that it is her nearly-beloved husband, has a moment of utter disappointment and frustration. His arms tighten around her, and she feels the arrogant prod of his erection against her thigh. Wife has attack of claustrophobia, feels the stifling suffocating arms of Spireslea closing around her, wants to scream but stifles it. He: 'I love you.' She (in despair) 'I know!'

And after he had polished off the remaining scraps from lunch, he wanted his oats and I lay there thinking of England - or rather, thinking how unlike a real man Graham is. Or perhaps I should have written, how unlike my fantasy man he is. My wished-for lover doesn't have an overflowing, hairy belly in which, if there are muscles, they are well buried in fat. Or a tufty chest with going-white mat of hair and vast nipples, like saucers. Or a two-chinned face, flabby and wet. Or a horrible penis...I feel so guilty writing this down! He's such a KIND man. Kind.

But it does sum up what I was feeling last night and I have to write down all my thoughts, even if they're wrong.

Afterwards he lay back, hands behind his head catching his breath. And then he asked me, 'What's the matter?'

I was startled for a moment. Graham is perceptive; yet I had thought that my performance was at least up to the usual standard. I know what is expected of me after all: when to pant, when to moan, when to fake orgasm. I have to do that rather a lot, because sex is very tiring and I know he won't let himself come until I do the oh! oh! - Oh! stuff. It shows what a NICE man he is. And then he can lie back with his smug 'aren't I *gooood* ' look and say something like 'God you're wonderful Mrs Alpert' and that's it. Thus do I earn my valium and delicious sleep.

'Nothing. Why?'

'You're not your usual self. What's the matter? Are you feeling bad?'

'A slight headache. Nothing.'

'Sex cures headaches.' He put an arm around me. 'You should feel fine now. But that's not it, is it?'

I felt a trace of annoyance. I wanted to sleep. 'I'm alright.' I said, trying to turn away against the restraint of his arm. It tightened.

'Tell me,' he said insistently.

'Nothing to tell,' I muttered.

'I see.' he said and let go. He must have been rather offended, because he crossed his arms on his chest, which allowed me to escape and turn over. 'It could be one of many things. One: you're really not feeling well and there's something you're not telling me. Did something happen at the hospital?' he paused for a reply. I stayed silent. 'Or two: you're upset because the money for the wendy-house hasn't gone into your account yet. I forgot. I promise to do it tomorrow.'

I reached for the valium bottle, unscrewed and popped.

'Three: you're unhappy here. Huh! But that isn't really possible is it? You have everything a woman could possibly need!...'

Please shut up, I thought, snuggling deeper under the duvet.

'Four: you don't really love me and you wish you were somewhere else...eh? Sally?'

Damn damn damn! I thought and with a supreme effort I turned around and hugged him hard. He freed his arms and then reciprocated with stifling sincerity.

'You're being silly, ' I murmured, 'Paranoid. I love you. Now go to sleep.'

And as the pills took me away for the night I remember thinking, Right on all Four Counts, you bastard, Right on all Four Counts...

*

Building this wendy-house seems to be an endless task. The windows are far from finished, and there's still the roof to pop on top of this absurd wooden box. Then the painting inside and out. Then we have to put tar stuff over the roof. And we'll have to furnish it! And curtain it. And carpet it. And put silk or plastic (!!) flowers on the windowsill...strange how, while my whole upbringing and all my childhood influences revolt against this innocent building, I seem to get some sort of feeling of fulfilment from its construction. The process of creating something which will last (at least a little longer than I will) (a sort of scratch in the sands of time, as Mother used to say, to be washed away no doubt by the first wave...)

The first of my builders arrived at ten. George, grin intact. And a few seconds later, Harry clattered in with more tools and an armful of wood.

'Hello there Mrs A,' Harry said. 'Carpentry day!' and he dropped the wood ceremoniously on the lawn.

'Morning workers,' I said cheerily. 'Tea?'

'Why not,' George chirped.

'Let's make a start while our host gets tea,' Harry suggested. 'Come on lad, if you want to be an apprentice you'll have to show willing! Work first, tea after.'

'I always thought the British worker did things the other way round,' George mused.

'Not in my platoon, old boy. Let's get cracking.'

I emerged from the house with a tea-tray half an hour later. The day was hot and cloudless, already muggy and stifling. The remains of yesterday's wind played with the treetops.

In deference to Harry's last pronouncement, I poured the tea out into mugs and took them to the workers. Harry was ripping out the window-frames George had installed yesterday, making loud patronising tutting noises. 'Not a proper job at all my boy, not a proper job. Nobody ever taught you how to do joints, that's obvious! Here, have a look Mrs A. Pretty amateurish, eh? Can you imagine what happens when water gets into this space, eh?'

I gave George a reassuring grin. 'Tut,' I said, 'Tut tut.'

'I'm not a carpenter Harry, I'm sorry!' George said, putting on a little-boy embarrassed look. 'What I need is a real expert like you to show me what's what.'

'Flattery eh? Well it always works on me.' He took a grateful sip of tea. 'Lovely!' he said with a smile.

George leaned against an unfinished wall and drank. 'So how are you today Sally?' he asked.

'I'm fine. And you seem to have recovered from your injury.'

'Yes I have, thanks to you.' he stroked a net of sticky plasters on his forearm.

'I'll have to train you how to use a damned saw properly, won't I? Damned stupid thing to do, that.' Harry said.

I felt a need to come to the wounded soldier's defence. 'Hang on a minute, he's a graphic designer, not a carpenter.'

'Well,' Harry said with strained jocularity, 'perhaps the boy should stick to what he knows!' and I realised that all his jolly banter hides some genuine antipathy. Racist?

I warmed to George again. My silly flaw: I always confuse feelings of protectiveness for Love! And George seemed to need protection from this bullying ex-army sergeant-major. I managed to keep my voice light. 'Come on Harry,' I reminded him 'it's very kind of George to offer to help.'

'Right! Quite right! Jolly good of the fellow. Well, let's get on, eh?'

I was dismissed, so I went back to the house to work out a shopping-list, tidy the bedroom, clear up the breakfast things, all of that.

Thinking, isn't it awful how the men and women seem to have fallen into sexually stereotypical roles in all this. As for me, I'm happy not to be carpentering...

I was busy in the kitchen when Harry came in. 'Sorry to disturb you,' he said, shuffling, 'a little awkward actually.'

'What? What's awkward?' I think I expected him to say that he refused to work with George.

'It's the money, actually,' he said with some embarrassment. 'I'm so sorry to have to talk about this. We're not rich, you see, Joan and me, both on a pension as you know, and all this stuff costs rather a lot, not to mention the expense of all the equipment we're going to have to buy. You must forgive me.'

'I understand - ' I said

'Joan's going round now, canvassing for dosh. Everybody promises, y'know, damn few pennies in all. We tell them the whole story, vows of silence and that, and you'd think they'd leap into action, chequebooks at the ready, but no. At least some offer help - like the chap out there...rum fellow, by the way.'

'Why rum?' I asked, ready for defensive action.

'Bit nancyboyish, if you know what I mean. Maybe it's just the fact he's a foreigner...'

'He was born here' I said, teeth gritted.

'Was he? Well...' luckily for him he decided not to pursue that line. 'Anyway, notwithstanding all that, do you think...?'

'You mean the money? That's no problem.' I reached for my chequebook, praying silently that Graham had remembered to transfer it from his account to mine. I wrote, handed the slip to him.

'A thousand pounds!' he said, delighted grin making his face all crackly. 'Excellent!'

*

I realise that all the stuff I've written tonight was a delaying tactic. I'm trying to stave off putting down what happened after that and I don't know why. Maybe I just want to draw out the pleasure, draw it out because I want to relive it.

Or is it shame?

Both. I can still smell him on my skin, it's a musty, muscly, sweet-sweat smell, and I don't want to ever wash it off.

So unlike Graham's smell! Which is sour and used and Paco Rabanne.

Here goes then:

In the afternoon I laid out a cold meat and salad lunch in the garden, as yesterday. George and Harry ate with me in the sun. Both had abandoned their shirts. Both so male! They seemed to take up the whole garden. Men occupy so much *space*!

And having them there made me feel flirtatious and light, basking in their attentions. They felt it too, and we did plenty of laughing and joshing and Harry managed to keep his interactions with George on a perfectly jolly level.

I'm rushing now!

Ah but mainly I was playing with George. Yesterday's feelings of withdrawal from him had been forgotten and I was back in fantasy mode. 'It's all only a movie,' I had decided. Only a movie.

'I do love being surrounded by handsome men,' I said.

'Hardly *surrounded* my dear. Harry grinned. 'There are only two of us. Besides, ' he added, looking at his watch, 'you'll be surrounded by only one of us in a minute. I have to pop off.'

'Oh,' I said, momentarily nonplussed, 'More important business?'

He tapped his nose. 'More recruits,' he said conspiratorially. 'Joan's set up something for this afternoon. We're growing fast.'

'That's good,' George said. 'Are you sure you trust me with the windows?'

'I've shown you how to do it, lad, that's all I can do. Eh? Just remember to keep those joints tight.'

'I will.' George grinned again and stared straight at me. I was lost in his eyes for a second.

I think that was what did it. Pushed me over the edge. I started shaking. I knew then what I was going to do.

When Harry stood up to go, pulling on his shirt, muttering about how he'd hate to be late I hardly noticed, though I expect I made the right noises...

And then he was gone leaving George and me, just George and me.

'Do you want a cup of tea?' I asked, hoping that my voice was firm.

'That would be nice' George answered and I went to the kitchen and put the kettle on.

Then I went up to the bedroom and dropped three Valium from the bottle into my hand. Then back to the kitchen, where I crushed them between two spoons and swooshed them into a cream with milk, which I added to his cup of tea. I was singing to myself, I can't remember what, probably 'One day my Prince will Come'

I was happy! So happy!

I couldn't believe I was doing this. Yet I didn't hesitate, I had no doubts at all.

So I gave him his Mickey Finn and we lay in the sun innocently chatting until, stretched out in the iron chair, George fell into deep sleep.

I was only then that I began to have flashes of doubt. Now what? Here before me this Sleeping Beauty, here at my mercy? Stretched out, arms hooked over the back of the chair, hips thrust out and wonderful torso gleaming with sweat in the sun...Now I've got it - I thought, - what am going to *do* with it?

I stood, breathing heavily and shaking slightly, and went over to the body. That's all you are now my fine George, just a body, a beautiful, live male body. Then I went behind the chair and, one arm around him for support (the first touch! -) I eased him down onto the patio, pulling the chair away. It was almost effortless.

The feel of his skin! It is smooth, so smooth, so silky and taut. Oh and he smells so *fine*! Sweet perspiration and another scent I can't identify.

I buried my nose in his armpit, and then ran my tongue, flickering across his chest. Circled the nipples with the tip, one after the other. The fine hairs tickled my teeth. Deliberately, slowly, I plucked a single hair from the chest. I must keep that...

Was there a slight change in his breathing? Was it getting heavier? I sat back to evaluate. But no, George was sleeping deeply, like a baby, like a big, drugged baby. I could do anything to him. Anything...

I bent to him again and adored his body with my hands, sliding my fingers up and down his chest and abdominals, up and around his arms, enjoying every mound and valley, then down that wonderful warm stomach and. And then over his belt and my tentative hand felt the crotch and

Iron! Steel! Pushing!

My fingers shaking I clumsily undid the belt and unbuttoned the jeans and I was right! There, beautiful, magnificent, climbing up!

My clothes came off I don't know how and I made myself wet and I wet him with spittle and sat astride, easing him into me, my legs going into almost uncontrollable shivers! it was exquisite, man at my command, passive, rampant man, aroused, insensible!

And afterwards I wasn't overcome with guilt, no, not at all! I was sort of - *proud*, you know? Proud. I felt I had worked for it and I deserved it. No, I don't think rape is right but - who exactly had been hurt? Besides, it's time women had some revenge...

*

I am convinced that when George woke (after having been washed and dressed by me) he had no idea that he had pleasured me as he slept. When he opened his eyes he found himself on the chair he had fallen asleep in, and his first sight was of me sewing curtains. I asked him if he had enjoyed a good nap, adding that I hated to have woken him. He looked so tired.

'Good lord,' he said, 'I feel wrecked. I'm so sorry. The effects of last night I suppose. What's the time?'

I knew then that I had gotten away with it! I let go a great releasing sigh. 'Five thirty.'

'Gosh, I cannot apologise enough. I must go. Tell that Harry when you see him I'm sorry I didn't finish the blasted window. I'll do it tomorrow...'

And he left me feeling like a queen bee, fat and bloated and smug and bloody satisfied. Gorged.

CHAPTER THREE

I've been thinking about AIDS again. What if I've been infected? Does it matter? (I've just realised: last page I said I'm going to die. Am I accepting that as a fact? Am I believing it?) The cancer could well kill me before the AIDS does.

But *what about Graham*? My rape - that's what I'm going to call it - mustn't be the death of Graham I can't leave him that as a legacy.

I don't know if George ejaculated or not. Surely he couldn't have? How can a man on three valium ejaculate? Come to think of it, how could a man on three valium have an erection? But even if he didn't *come*, and he had the disease I could have caught it. Damn! I was so carried away at the time, I forgot! If only I had slipped a condom onto him! I don't have a condom. I couldn't have done it, even if I had one. I was too mad.

If I carry the virus I must not give it to Graham. God I feel so despairing. NOW I feel guilty. Though still not ashamed, though perhaps I should be.

It means I can't let Graham make love to me.

That's what it means.

He'll be off to Japan in a few days. If I can just keep him off me until then! How the hell am I going to do that? I could suggest we use condoms. No I couldn't. What reason could I give? It would imply that I knew one of us had been unfaithful. I'm in trouble. Deep trouble.

*

The last few days have been hell. That's why I haven't written anything. I must write it all down now, so that you will understand why I have reached my decision. I am trapped, trapped. I have trapped myself into a course of action which will be seen as cruel and stupid, yet it's what I *want* to do.

Graham couldn't understand why I refused him. I realised that I couldn't give illness as an excuse, it'd make him worry and he'd cancel his trip, and that wouldn't do.

So I just refused, invented reasons to argue, brought up every monster we have in our closets. We argued, bickered, fought every night to give me the excuse I needed to give him cold shoulder after cold shoulder. Then I'd take two valium, knowing that Graham is too much of a gentleman to take me sleeping...unlike me!

And I began to believe in my anger with him. I played my part so well. How dare he shut me up in this house, away from my friends and the things I love - like theatre, music, going out. How dare he tell me that he chose the entire decor with me in mind when he bought the house ready-made, like a suit at C&A. In fact, how dare he assume that the tacky trash in this house would make me happy, assume I have no taste? Didn't he realise that he and I were as incompatible as could be, that we have nothing in common...why did he steal me from Barry, a man I loved, who protected me even though he would never marry me?

And...and...and!

Yes I feel guilty. I hurt him so much. But I do have anger, real anger. I'm angry at everything! Not just Graham my jailer but the Cancer! And me! And the Cancer!

It's not fair it's not FAIR NOT...stop writing stop writing STOP WRITING

*

Sorry about that. I'm back now and I feel a little better. I promised to put it all down, and that's what I'm going to do. I will control myself. RESOLUTION: I will control myself and not fall into mawkish sentimental self pity. I will limit my anger and just tell the story.

The story: On Tuesday, Joan came to tell me that the Meeting (which I had forgotten to attend) went very well. 'Dozens more recruits dear, dozens! Every soul on the Estate will keep their eyes on the dreadful Tweeds, they'll not be able to move without being reported. We're a jolly Foggy army! ' Ah, so that was why George hadn't turned up. Boy! Wuz I scared!

'That's very good,' I said.

'I'm not one to pry dear, but we did expect you. What happened?'

'I - wasn't feeling well,' I said.

'What was it? That twenty four hour 'flu? Everyone's had it. Such a nuisance.'

Which reminded me that perhaps I should have told her about my illness. It creates vast possibilities for excuses.

'Must have been,' I said.

'And the wendy-house isn't far from finished, is it? We're going to have to develop an Early Warning System once it's in operation. You see, if we can man it twenty four hours - shifts of course - and monitor everything that goes on in that house - as soon as we get the slightest whiff of anything suspicious we can be in there like the SAS, every man - and woman jack of us.'

I shook my head as if trying to free it of cobwebs. Suddenly I realised how crazy this is all getting. Up to now it all seemed like a game, annoying but harmless. But I had this moment, you see, of utter clarity. Like a vision. Of how ridiculous we are. Especially Joan. Her plottings and schemings. Her absurd Machiavellian airs. And I wanted to laugh.

'Joan ...this is all...mad. Mad.'

'I feel that too, sometimes,' she said with a grin that disarmed me. 'But then I remind myself that a child's life is at stake, do you see? An *innocent* child.'

'Her mother doesn't think she's so innocent,' I said.

'The woman who *calls* herself her mother.' Joan corrected me like a school mistress. 'You wouldn't take *that* woman's word for anything would you?'

'No of course not' I said, to mollify her. But then, remembering Jean Tweed's words of the day before...(I forgot to mention: Jean Tweed saw my Rape. She saw! From an upper window. Wait, let me finish this part then I'll tell you about that.) I could hate that woman quite easily. And I realised that I'd much prefer to believe anything this big warm round barrel of a countrywoman says than that pompous bitch next-door.

'Well I'm glad to hear it. We have your subscription by the way, do we?' She asked, as she prepared to leave.

'Subscription?' I echoed dimly.

'I forgot for a moment that you weren't at the meeting. That's what we're calling it. The thousand pounds for joining the Foggies. We need lots of money, dear, to save that child.'

'Yes,' I said, 'I gave Harry a cheque.'

'Good good,' she said.

Back to the subject of the Tweed. Yes, I do believe I hate her now. You see, I had to find out if Annie (I'm still calling her Annie. I may start calling her Mary Dyne soon.) will still be in hospital when I'm admitted. And if so, I'd have to tell her some sort of lie about why I'll be there. This was Wednesday morning.

So I went to the King Edward at around ten, knowing that I could charm the nurses if necessary into allowing me to visit. I hoped I'd be able to get in and out before Madam Tweed arrived.

The girl greeted me enthusiastically and I gave her the book I'd bought on the way. It was not a romance. It was a garishly jacketed copy of Stevenson's 'Kidnapped'.

'Gosh,' she said as she pulled the volume out of its paper bag, 'it looks very juicy. I haven't read this. I'm sure I'll enjoy it.' She didn't sound entirely convincing. 'Good title anyway.' She smiled, perky chin creasing like an old potato.

I asked my question.

'A couple of weeks I think. That depends on when they decide I'm ready. Honestly, they're so vague here.'

'I'm sorry to hear that. I'm going to be in their vague care from Monday.'

'Really? Why?' she asked.

'Nothing serious. A little treatment, a few investigations' I felt, after all, a reluctance to lie to her.

She accepted this as sufficient explanation and appeared to lose interest. 'How nice,' she said vaguely. 'It'll be good for me having you nearby.'

'You know,' I said thoughtfully, 'it could be very useful if you weren't discharged before me.'

'Why?' she asked absently.

She wasn't taking me seriously enough. I decided to sound mysterious and urgent. 'In fact,' I said sotto voce, 'it could be Important.' And I gave her an Important look.

Finally she asked Why? again.

'Um - well, we don't want you back home until we're - uh - ready. We're mounting a surveillance unit. To protect you.'

'Gosh!' she said, impressed.

'That's right', I said, almost believing myself. 'We have to get all the equipment together. We're going to fit all sorts of - things.'

She leaned forward excitedly. 'You mean like secret cameras and microphones and bugs and things?'

'Exactly.'

'Bugs? Are there *bugs* in the hospital?' I looked up. The cheery, plummy voice belonged to Joan Tweed.

'Good morning!' Annie said, surprisingly cheerful.

'Hello dear. I was just shopping so I popped in with a few grapes.' She was dressed in a smart grey-brown suit, a loud and cheerful blue and red silk scarf with butterflies around neck and shoulders. She carried a Harrods carrier bag, obviously much used.

'Good morning,' I said, trying to be friendly.

She twitched as if I'd stung her with a peashooter. 'Were you serious about bugs?' she asked Mary (from this moment I'm going to call her Mary.)

'Oh it's just a rumour,' Mary said.

'You said bugs,' she was obviously trying to find out whether Mary had used the word in a literal or figurative sense. She was full of suspicion.

'She was talking about cockroaches,' I said.

She ignored me. 'I asked, ' this to Mary, 'what *sort* of bug?'

'What Sally says,' Mary answered sullenly.

'I wish you wouldn't talk to that woman!' Tweed snapped. She was breathing heavily with suppressed anger.

'What?' Mary asked.

'*That* woman. The one who keeps interfering.'

'Do you mean Sally? She's not *that* woman. She's my friend!'

All I could see of the Tweed was her back, but I could imagine the expression on her face. Bitter and toothclenched, mouth twisted with disgust and loathing as she said 'That woman. That...*adulteress*!'

The word came at me like one of those horrible Japanese martial-art weapons full of scything whirring blades, and it hit me in the chest.

'That's rubbish!' Mary cried loud enough to call scurrying nurses and wake sleeping patients. 'You're being stupid! She's my friend!'

'You don't believe me? Oh I assure you it's true. I saw it myself! With that foul pretty boy from number 32. On her patio, in broad daylight! Shameless! Disgusting!'

I was frozen, stuck to the chair. Had I been able to stand, I would have made a run for it.

'She would never do that! She's too much of a mouse. She loves her husband...Sally, *tell* her!'

I couldn't say a word.

'Believe me, I saw it! And I can't have you having an adulteress for a friend. She'll pollute you!'

'Is it true, Sally, is it?' Mary pleaded.

I still couldn't move, couldn't speak. The woman Who Stopped. Like a clock. Stopped. Showing nothing but expressionless dial.

'I'm going shopping now,' Tweed announced. 'I'll be half an hour. And I don't want that woman there when I get back. And we can have a *proper* visit.'

Then she swept out past me, dropping the grapes on the bed as she went.

I sat glued.

Mary stared at me. 'I say,' she said breathlessly, 'How *exciting*!'

*

Exciting for me, all right. Especially if that woman gets it into her head to tell Graham.

Nightmare. Two days to go. Two more days to live through and then he's off, away for two weeks...

CHAPTER FOUR

All my worst nightmares have come true. That hypocritical harridan, that mean and damaged woman has told Graham.

I'm fairly calm now, though I wasn't last night. I was shaking and crying and riven by guilt. And Graham was so quiet, calm, reasonable.

Bastard! If only he'd accused, raved, shouted.

He came home early, gravitas sitting on his face like pancake makeup. He didn't kiss me hello, and I knew then. He said he wanted to talk. He fixed himself a stiff brandy and gave me a Cinzano, without asking whether I wanted it. Then he invited me, very politely, to sit in the armchair. And faced me, sitting on the couch. The fake Regency coffee table between us for protection.

'I know,' he said sadly.

Without hope I asked, 'What.'

'I know about number 32.' he said. Then he sighed deeply and I knew that from now on we would be in cliché land. Spireslea's so typical Cliché Land.

'I see,' I said, deciding that sticking to the script would be easiest.

He took a deep draught of the brandy, then topped up his glass. 'How long has this been going on?' he asked.

'Oh,' I said, 'not long.'

'I see,' he said.

I felt a hole filled with misery opening under me. 'I - ' I nearly blurted, I'm so sorry, it was a one-off, I won't do it again - but I couldn't say the words.

I knew what the next question would be. And it was. 'Is it serious?' he asked.

I hesitated a second before saying 'Yes...I think so.' I don't know why I said that. Or do I.

'I see.' he said again. 'Well, I've already had a word with Peter, ' the lawyer, 'and if you want a divorce there'll be no problem from my side.'

My turn to say 'I see.'

George is down in the garden as I write this, knocking nails into timber on the patio. He just waved at the window. He's shirtless and grinning. I feel as if he's mocking me.

I want to finish writing this scene. I have to tidy the house. I have to expend *lots* of energy. I will hoover and dust savagely. I will polish everything, as if I can make my life clean and shiny.

Scour out the past!

And then, perhaps, I will Stop. Just freeze...how would it be if one day I went out, say to the town, and stood in a doorway. And stopped, just stopped. Closed down. Allowed catatonia.

I wonder if there's any alternative.

I'll carry on: Graham explained, very reasonably, that he'd make all the necessary financial arrangements. I would have everything I need. He would leave me in possession of the house. (Not that, please not that)

Then he said, quite rightly, 'You're being very silly you know.'

And even though he was right, his patronising arrogance annoyed me. 'Am I.' I said.

'It's not unusual for a woman of your age - sorry to bring that up, to seek consolation with a younger man. Not unusual at all. But it never lasts.'

'Is that so.' I said.

'I think you should use the fortnight I'm away to think about it. You must consider everything. Explore your relationship with this toy boy, this bimbo - does he know about your illness? - I'm sorry,' he felt the need to apologise for his brief show of emotion. Then his tone changed and he whined 'I don't understand, I really don't! I'm trying to understand. I mean how could you prefer that - that - to me? Aren't I loving enough? We've always had good sex, until the last few days anyway - '

'*You* did, ' I said.

'What?'

'*You* had good sex.'

'But you always - !'

'I can't stand this...' I said.

'I've given you everything. Everything.' We were reverting to script. 'Whatever you wanted. A dream house, garden, beautiful countryside, enough money to have a wonderful life...'

'Did you ever ask *me* what *I* wanted?' We were getting back to last night's subject. Old ground.

'I stood by you, right through your illness - '

Ah, so it came out at last. He went straight for the heart. And I ran out of the room, up the stairs, threw myself onto the bed and sobbed, inconsolable.

...as I said, I'm calmer now. Graham will be home soon, I dread seeing his blank face, I dread the politeness we will show each other.

I wonder if what I'm doing subconsciously is driving Graham away, so that he won't have to live through the pain of seeing me die.

I suppose *why* doesn't matter really.

So long as I do my bit to save Mary Dyne before I go. Then, nothing matters. And it's better for Graham this way.

*

The last day before Graham goes away. Hey. A line from a poem. It feels as if something is lifting from my shoulders, a big deep unwanted weight. Yet I'm still in the woods, still deep in trouble. So why do I feel so light and cheery? The sun is shining, George is outside working, - 'helped' by Mary McCarthy, who's on half-term.

What a strange old turnip she is. Her body - which is, as I said, turnip-shaped - encased in spring flowers. She's wearing a head scarf, as if to protect her greasy hair from any chance of sun pollution. And sandals.

George was almost - flirtatious? - when they arrived to start work. Grinning at me like a mischievous little boy sharing an unspoken secret...he can't know! If he did he would have - what. What would he have done? I know what I would have done. Screamed rape. Visited police. Gone crazy.

I wonder if Graham will say anything to him. God that would be absurd! I can imagine the scene: Act 2: Cuckolded husband, having extracted confession from wife, knocks on lover's door. 'I need to talk to you. About Hermione.'

'Ah yes, do come in. Is she ill?' "Lover" ushers husband into gay love-nest, walls covered in portraits of undressed young men.

Husband stares at decor, swallows his apprehension, says 'I know about your affair with her and I want to ask you if it's serious.'

'What?? What affair??' stunned "lover" asks, utterly confused.

Ha ha ha hee hee. Oh I must go downstairs, talk to the workers, give them tea, make them happy.

*

That's what I did. There is no doubt that George remains in ignorance of his heterosexual experience. I'm delighted. In fact he's as friendly and cheerful as ever. I'm beginning to think of him as cute again.

The McCarthy is perfectly revolting. It's not just that I'm bored by her greenness or frustrated by her militant PC. It's her assumption that she's the only person for miles who appreciates these values. She doesn't need to preach to *me*! But it's no good telling her that, she obviously feels that she's the only person who truly understands all the injustices in the world and as such it's her job to keep her back against the wall and rant at passers-by.

Also there's her constant use of the 'We women...' phrase, which she employs to try and force me into alliance, though no doubt she is convinced that I'm far too repressed and stupid to understand.

'We women,' she said, sipping her tea aggressively, 'have to organise everything in the end. This is because of the basic fact that most men are totally incompetent.' She glared a challenge at George, who nodded, smiled, winked. 'Take Joan Bellings. Wonderful woman. Without her none of this would have happened - ' She gestured toward the part-finished wendy-house as if it was a new Home for Oppressed Women.

'We're going to put the roof on next,' George said, trying to divert her from this wearisome path.

'That's excellent!' I said, joining in the conspiracy. 'Once that's done we can finish decorating...'

'We've been so lucky with the weather' he smiled.

'The farmers, I'm sure, wouldn't agree' McCarthy said belligerently.

'Perhaps not,' George said, determined not to get into an argument with the woman. I suspect they've already had more than one disagreement.

'Where's the Major?' I asked. 'I haven't seen Harry for a few days now.'

'Aha,' George said. 'Gone to London with Joan to buy all the equipment. They must have collected enough money by now.'

'Really?' I must admit that a funny thought flashes through the mind as I write this: Are the Old Foggies lovers? What an amazing idea!

'Typical isn't it' McCarthy said.

'What?' I asked, mystified.

'You can't trust the forces of law and order to protect citizens of this country any more. The fact that we - private people - have to spend all this money on doing the state's job...it's the same in education nowadays. In my school now...'

I really didn't want to hear, though I can't help agreeing. It's just that I can't bear to hear this woman mouthing things I believe in. It pollutes them. 'Oh dear,' I said meaningfully, 'time to put the kettle on again!' And I dashed into the kitchen and made loud noises to drown out her voice.

Returned with a fresh pot of tea. Then (anything to change the subject) I said casually, 'By the way, I forgot to mention, I'll be going into hospital on Monday, for a week or two.'

'Really?' George was genuinely concerned. 'What's the matter?'

'Oh, nothing serious,' I said, resorting to the female safe area, 'Women's' Problems.' I said it to prevent his asking more questions, but of course it had the reverse effect on McCarthy.

'Womb is it? Tubes? '

Uncomfortably I answered, 'That sort of thing.'

'I had so much trouble myself. It's amazing how society expects women to bear children and take on the burdens we have to when there are so many things that can go wrong. Men can never understand that, never! The greatest problem they face regularly with their bodies is scraping their brute hair off their chins every morning. Now me, I had a hysterectomy when I was 36, 36 can you imagine, still good-looking, still able to be a good mother. I was devastated at the time of course. But thank heavens now I'm older I realise how free that operation made me. No man can hold me to ransom you see. Tie me to their house and car and force me to stay in a cage with a yapping brood of children. I do what I want you see. Free as a bird me..' She sat back smugly, happy to have proven her infinite superiority to George, me and the rest of the human race.

Yes, I thought, I dislike you a great deal, fat woman, but you may just have a point there. (It's strange how so many people who share my beliefs are so... revolting...)

'We'd better get back to work,' George said and drained his tea. Giving me a lovely opportunity to admire the shape of his shoulder, the superb twitching curl of the bicep, as he raised the mug to his thirsty lips.

'You'd better leave us the keys to this house then Sally, if you and your man are to be away,' McCarthy said, organising us.

I agreed happily to this plan.

'And by the time you get out we'll be ready to start surveillance operations,' George said with a narrow smile. 'It sounds so cloak and dagger, doesn't it?'

'At least you can keep an eye on the girl while you're in there, Sally', McCarthy said. 'Best if she stays in hospital until we're finished. Otherwise anything can happen.'

'True,' I said, 'I had thought of that. 'I must explain this more carefully to Mary Dyne. Even if she has to fake she must stay until everything's ready...I just can't face the Wicked Stepmother again. I will have to be careful about timing my visits.

*

Graham's gone. Pheeew. His dark and heavy presence is no longer on my shoulders, his hangdog eyes no longer seeking mine. I feel really free!

And tomorrow I go into hospital, a rich woman.

You see, poor Graham had been trying to make amends. Yesterday he transferred some money into my bank account. Perhaps he's been talking to the McCarthy.

I think I'd better tell you about last night, when we sat down to what I had decided would be a deliberately Unspecial meal.

'We'd better talk business,' he said.

I had been steeling myself for this Last Supper, taken a valium with my handful of pills. (If you want to know: Antibiotics, antifungal tablets - which I have to dissolve and swish around my mouth - nutritional supplements, and the odd pain-killer; a total of twenty seven pills) I was feeling sullen, emotionless. 'All right,' I said.

'I've been thinking a great deal about us.'

'So have I.'

'And I've concluded that I have been a little - unfair, I suppose is the word.' He raised his eyebrows, hoping for a denial.

I obliged. 'No no,' I said, 'I'm sure you've been trying your best.'

'Perhaps I've been trying too hard,' he said. He was picking distractedly at the tasteless chicken. 'I've never given you any freedom, have I.'

'Freedom...' I said wonderingly.

'I have decided to transfer £5,000 to your bank account.'

'Have you?'

'Give you some financial independence. It's what you want isn't it?'

'Yes', I answered, trying to avoid showing the resentment I feel at his never having done this before.

'And when I come back, if you still want to live with me, we'll move house. You choose the house, you buy the furniture, you arrange the decorating. I'll leave everything in your hands.'

'Really?' I asked, not believing all this.

'Yes,' he said, 'really. I do want you to be happy and I realise that you're not. That's the reason you decided to have this - *fling* thing.' His eyes went down to the salad, and his fork-finger shook.

I sighed. 'But you still don't understand, do you?'

'I don't!' He met my eyes briefly. Then involved himself in the transfer of lettuce from plate to stomach.

'I mean,' I realised how cruelly my last statement had sounded. 'I want us *both* to be happy. We should have a home where we're both happy, surrounded by things both of us like...' I glanced around at the familiar Spirescape of the 'dining area'. 'If only that were possible...'

'I'm sure it's possible.' Graham detected a ray of hope. 'I can compromise. And I'm sure you can too. We'll come to an agreement.'

'Oh Graham...' I said, feeling the ghost of a trace of pity for this gawky, hulking man who loves me.

'I don't even care if you go on seeing that boy. No, don't say anything. As long as I don't know anything about it...and,' he added with the semblance of a grin, 'as long as none of the *neighbours* know anything either...'

I wasn't able to smile at that.

'I love you Sally, that's my problem,' he said sadly, eyes moist. Then he reached across the table, nudging the soggy instant meal out of the way.

I hope you will understand why I could not avoid taking his proffered hands, even though mine were shaking.

'Will you make love with me tonight?' he asked, looking me straight in the eyes. I nodded, God forgive me, with the Rolling Stones' lyric going through my head: *This could be the Last Time,/ This could be the Last time,/ May be the last time, I don't know....Oh no!'* all mixed up with guilt and sorrow...what am I doing to this good, harmless man? But the problem is: he can't be the man I need.

And we made love. Graham pulled a condom out of his pocket very ashamedly, like a teenager on his first date. 'I - ' he started to explain, but I stopped his mouth. 'It's all right Graham,' I said.

(I helped him put it on. What a fuss. He doesn't seem to have used one before, or was that an act? No, I don't think so. He was all fumbly and said ow a few times as the thing captured tiny hairs and tried to pull them out. But I unrolled it determinedly over his going-flaccid penis. Oh but I soon got him hard! For the first time in my life I let a penis into my mouth, albeit encased so I couldn't taste it...instead,

I tasted the infuriatingly bitter spermicide with which the thing was coated and I nearly gagged. It is the worst taste I have ever had to endure, worse even than Pulmo's Bailly...yet, and I'm very proud of myself for this, I managed to go on licking and nibbling until he was absolutely hard, and then I guided him into me, thinking of George coming in, so hard and relentless - and Graham let me ride him as hard as I had ridden George and I loved it! It's the first time I have ever really *enjoyed* sex with Graham. As opposed to enjoying the fact that he was enjoying himself. And with my eyes closed I didn't have to look down at the hairy heaves and rolls of his belly, he could have been anyone...)

*

Now the only big thing I have to go through is the treatment. I do hope it works, I don't want scalpels near me. I am pretty tired, too little sleep last night, too disturbing to have a man in my bed all aroused and reaching out for me every few minutes to stifle me with his hot chest.

I had better go and pack my Hospital Kit. Which nightie? One that opens easily, in front preferably, so I don't have to remove the thing completely every time they examine me. (I will *not* wear their Official Inmate gowns. No!).

Toothbrush toothpaste moisturiser powder baby oil pills? Sanitary towels? Should I shave my legs? Decisions decisions.

BOOK III

CHAPTER ONE

WEDNESDAY

This place is so disorganised! Dr Jennings is supposed to be in charge of my case, right? Well she (Cathy) is calm and warm and reassuring but seems to have no influence at all on what they're going to do to me. And what's worse, she doesn't appear to understand the options. When she came to see me an hour or so after I had settled myself into the bed (thinking, how silly, going to bed mid-morning) all she said was, 'Don't worry dear. You're in the best possible hands here you know.'

'But what happens now, Cathy? When do I start the chemotherapy?'

'Oh it's far too early to start talking about that, dear. Just be patient...'

'No pun intended.'

'Certainly not!' She said with a laugh. 'Just make yourself comfortable and do whatever they tell you to do. All right?' She asked, patting me on the cheek.

'If you say so,' I said, and she left me in confusion.

It was two o'clock by the time the Oncologist, Dr Maister (I call him Doc Monster), called. He's a dark and looming Jewish doom person, who said 'I'm not sure we can reverse this cancer. It looks too advanced. I want you to have a scan. Don't get your hopes up.'

He was so miserable and depressed. I suppose dealing with all these dying people is just the sort of thing that would depress a person. Or maybe he has an unhappy home-life.

Anyway, as you can well imagine, I was left in a sink of terror and self-pity until the early evening when the radiologist, Dr Patel, came in. He's another very tall man, very self-assured, confident, reassuring. And he said 'You're not to worry. We're going to give you intensive radiotherapy, every day. The tumours will shrink. This sort of treatment is very successful in the vast majority of cases.'

So who am I to believe? The sister, for example? (A big, beautiful, blowsy black woman with a wonderful West Indian accent) When I came in she promised to arrange a massage for the afternoon. 'You'll be feelin sore all over onless we mek you soft,' she said, and when the afternoon arrived the physio didn't, 'Oh no me dear,' Sister said as if I had been very stupid to ask, 'that's *tomorrow*, physio day!'

Pills have just arrived, wheeled in by the nurse. I think I'll read for a while.

THURSDAY

And now it's tomorrow and no Physio (unless they work after seven?). The same thing will no doubt happen with Counselling. The Sister suggested that I would benefit from a 'good heart-to-heart' and I had to agree. It would help to talk to someone about what I feel about dying, to talk about my fears to a stranger.

I've just asked Sister. 'The Counsellor is sick,' she said. 'Won't be in all the week.' No explanation about the Physio, just, 'I'll find out.'

...This is a Private Ward. Graham will get the bill. It's supposed to be for two patients, but as the bed next to me is empty I have a nice big room to myself. There is a tiny television suspended in a corner high up, so that it hurts my neck to watch it. I have books and magazines (the magazines are the bored-middle-class type of periodical, supplied by some charity or other. They are obsessed with sex and clothes, which annoys and bores me in that order. How to Keep your Man. Stunning Autumn Shades. Oral Sex: Who Needs It? And housekeeping: Make Your Man Burn With A

Flambé ...I think I'll read that...what a load of tosh!

(The books are my good old friends like Henry James, Doris Lessing, Salinger...what's this? Oops, Patricia Highsmith.)

They won't let me do anything for myself at all, I don't know why. Am I that sick? I have to ring this bell when I want to go to the toilet, and a nurse wheels a potty-chair in...

Nobody seems able to answer any of my questions about what treatment they're planning, or when, or how. Or when the scan is to be. Or why. Or whether I'm dying or not. Or why...bugger it, they want me to eat now...

That was the sort of food that most people would label 'acceptable', but my stomach wasn't interested. (Dry breast of chicken, broccoli, a lump of cauliflower, a baked potato).

I'm very bored. The TV page informs me that there is absolutely nothing I could even bear to watch as mental wallpaper...I could do with a visitor, somebody who likes me.

I realise yet again that I have no real friends here. If I was in Bristol, there'd be plenty of people who would come and see me. Though thinking about it, when I was in that horrible Barry-thing I lost so many of my student mates. Few of them liked him, for some reason. By the time I ditched Barry (or he ditched me) there were only two left, Barbara and Tammy. And they were so wound up in their own relationships, I hardly saw them at all. (I'm lying. I know why they didn't like him: because he was married, and they didn't trust him to do the 'right thing', whatever that was. And they were right.)

I haven't even spoken to either of them on the telephone for the last six months.

No friends...except for the Foggies!

And - of course, there's Mary-Dyne...Mary Dyne! With all these life-death things going on I forgot all about... I'll ring the switchboard, find out...

Yes, she's still here. We've just had a long, whispered, conspiratorial conversation. Rather like two teenagers in adjoining beds at boarding school after lights-out. She's faking pain furiously, won't let the medics lay a hand on her. They want to remove the cast and she won't allow it. She says they're going to do more x-rays on Monday to try and find the cause of all this pain. Good girl! Good, good girl.

I wish I had George's number. There's still no reply from Joan's 'phone, I suppose she's still in London. I don't have Harry's number. Do I want to speak to those people? Do I really want them visiting, fussing over me to show what good friends they are? They know I'm in here, I suppose I am in danger of a visit...at least from George?

FRIDAY

It's Friday and they've started my radiation treatment already. I could have sworn Dr Patel said they'd start on Monday. Are these drugs clouding my brain? He said they needed to do bursts for five days at a time. Are they going to carry on over the weekend? I doubt it.

I'm beginning to doubt if they know what they are doing. This was reinforced this morning when Doc Monster came in with an entourage of little monsters (students I suppose.) 'This woman,' he said as if referring to an inanimate object, 'is suffering from relapsed Lymphoma.' he consulted the chart at the end of the bed briefly and fussily. 'Yes. Hm.' Then he glanced at me with a snapped 'Good morning Mrs - ' consulted his sheet 'Alpert. Alright this morning?'

'Fine,' I said.

'We're giving local radiation to the affected areas' he was talking to the students again, 'before considering chemotherapy. We'll do an ultrasound, CAT and Gallium next week, test liver and kidney functions. Then we'll go for MOPP. Any questions?'

I raised my hand. 'Please sir, I have a question,' I said with a silly grin.

'I'm sure you do,' he said. 'We can talk later.' He turned with a quick, exasperated movement, to the students. 'Come now ladies and gentlemen. Any questions!'

I wasn't to be put off. 'Please please!' I said, waving my hand in the air like one of my erstwhile pupils.

'Can't it wait?' he snapped.

'If I *do* wait ' I said, 'my chances of seeing you again through the weekend are rather slim. I know how busy you are...' I added to mollify him a little.

'Very well then. What is your question?'

'It's a *prognosis* I want. One doctor tells me that radiation will clear my problem up. You weren't too keen on it, the last time we talked. You're telling these people that after you use it you're going to do MOPP. That's chemotherapy isn't it? I mean...'

He nodded impatiently. 'So what precisely is your question?'

'I need to know what's going to happen. I mean, do I have six months or six years? Or more? I need to know this.'

He sighed, shrugged. I'm certain he is wholly without compassion. 'I can't answer you because I don't know the answer. It all depends on how effective the treatment is.'

'Come on, 'I said encouragingly, 'Six months or six years. Which would you bet on?'

'I wouldn't place money on either,' he said. 'You'll certainly last six months, though I doubt if you'll be around in six years...having said that, some people respond well, and I wouldn't rule out complete remission, though it is somewhat unlikely. There. Does that satisfy you?'

'Not really, ' I said, 'though it will have to do.'

'Good!' he said. Then, 'They'll be taking you for your first treatment in a half-hour or so, so you had best prepare yourself.'

*

I feel as if I must make some kind of intimate, detailed record of everything, as if I'm collecting evidence. I don't know why. Thought: if I'm not going to hang about until I'm old, am I merely trying to scratch my name into Time, like the child who carves his name in the school desk? Like Mother and her line on the beach?

As I used to point out to them, there are far better ways to ensure immortality! After all, desks are regularly replaced (or rather they used to be, when LEAs used to have some money for education), and then 'DAMIEN WOZ ERE' will be consigned to rot and be forgotten.

I loved those children. It was, after all, a rather exceptional school where I held my first and last post. (The last post: Taruuuum, taruuum, tarum ta ta TUM, tarummm..)

I sometimes think I'm going mad. It could be the drugs. I'm going to call Nurse so that I can have a pee...

*

That was....

I realise that there IS the Shadow, nagging me, tapping me on my left shoulder, Hey! And this, I must *now* admit, is why I'm writing this.

(She sighed, stretched, made some half-repressed moans of utter frustration, boredom, apprehension, drug-induced confusion, and wrote: dredging up memories of the past because the present is so damned *slow*.)

A Voluntary-aided Church of England Comprehensive school for 500 girls and boys aged twelve to eighteen in Bedminster just outside Bristol. Should I name it? (Choice: invent name close to real, or No Name At All.)

The Head-Teacher: Mr Chips, years later. Greyed now, with an air of cynical indifference and a reputation as an absolute bastard. By the time I left I had winkled out his secret: he loved every child in his care. Loved! So much so that he was unable to be kind to any, for fear that any moment his crust would crack and he'd hug and cry and then what. I'm not implying that he loved them *sexually*, I think it was even sadder than that. He had no children of his own, and it was all to do with an unfulfilled longing to be a father.

His poor wife was quite mad; on the few occasions we used to see her at school functions she'd sit stolidly in her allocated chair, eyes cast down (even if she was there to watch a play) as if in shame. I don't know quite what ailed her, though I think now she could have been Autistic, which would explain quite a lot of things...hm.

The Deputy Head (another man, see!) was my Barry, the man who played me like a fish for four years. Every now and then donating his prick to my crotch, as a temporary loan which he expected me to be eternally grateful for.

I know this is hard to believe in modern Britain but under Paul Masters' headship discipline was almost absolute. We had few if any rebel kids despite the fact that many came from poor estates around the place, and the atmosphere was happy, constructive, loving. I sure fell on my feet when I got that job! What a contrast with the schools I did my Teaching Practice in! In which hate-filled small people expressed their lack of hope in their futures by engaging in determined campaigns to drive teachers over the edge.

*

When I was appointed, I had entertained a very secret suspicion (hope?) that perhaps the place would turn me Christian. I regarded this possibility with apprehension (my parents were committed atheists, humanists, squishy Kennedy Liberals); though it would be so easy to dissolve into the comfortable arms of a two-thousand year old establishment, with words of comfort for every occasion.

What a disappointment...the more garbage I listened to in assemblies, the more I spoke to other teachers who were involved in the Church, the more I realised these things: that this religion is, just as Father used to say, a farrago of tales fit for children and fools, constructed by a hegemony which is orientated to money power and control, based on lies, more lies, based on the truth.

And the final proof there is no God is Cancer.

So what? So I know that there is no point in praying to a Supreme Being, because even if there were such a thing, he's made too many mistakes to be any real help.

It's such a PITY!

Hang on, they've arrived to take me downstairs...

*

They kept me hanging around in the radiation suite area for nearly an hour! Sitting in the wheelchair, nothing to do, nothing to read.

The treatment itself is painless, no problem. It seems no different to what I had before - surely they didn't have to admit me for this? I could easily have been treated as an outpatient?

Either it has something to do with my being Private, or they know something they're not telling me.

Flash of paranoia. Where is Cathy? I need to ask her things, she always explains everything so well. Plus she knows me, respects me enough to tell me the truth.

NOTE: Find out everything about MOPP. What Mopp. Mop up disease? What does MOPP stand for.

*

I 'phoned the answering machine to get my messages. Graham, 'Well I'm here, and very tired. Where are you?...Sally? Are you there? No. I'll 'phone tomorrow. Don't 'phone me, it's too expensive. Bye.'

And then another one. 'Hello Sally, where are you? I need to speak to you. I've been thinking a lot. I'll call again.'

AND another. 'I'm annoyed now. I suppose you're spending all your time with the toyboy. Well I'm still your husband and I think you should call me. Never mind the expense. Or perhaps I've got the time difference wrong...'

So, reluctantly, I asked the switchboard to get me the number. 'Yokohama - in Japan?' a young girl's voice with a heavy Midlands accent asked excitedly. 'Of course! Yes I will!'

I lay back and waited. Five minutes. Ten. Turned the TV on. The 'phone rang. 'Sally? It's Graham.' His voice sounded far too near. 'You've woken me up.'

'I'm terribly sorry - ' I said.

'What are you doing in hospital? Why didn't you tell me? What's happened? Should I come home?'

Damn! That woman blew the gaff. 'No, don't do that. It's nothing. Just tests.'

'Is it? Are you lying to me? For God's sake Sally '

'I'm not lying, Graham! Listen! It's only tests. I'll be out next week. There's absolutely no reason for you to come home.'

'Only tests?' his near-panic slightly calmed, 'I knew you weren't well, I *knew*...'

'Graham I'm fine, really.'

'Really?' he asked. 'Well, I do hope you're not lying to me...this Conference is rather important, it'll help my image to be here. But if you're not well you'll have to tell me straight away.'

'Of course I will.'

'I want to speak to your doctor. Where's your doctor?'

That was a good question. I haven't seen one all day. 'I don't know. It's seven-thirty at night, I suppose they've gone home.'

'I'll 'phone the hospital tomorrow. Then I'll decide what to do.'

'You do that.' I said.

'I - uh - I love you, you know.'

I didn't know how to reply to that. 'Thank you very much,' I said.

*

Immediately after dropping the telephone I lifted it again. 'Tammy? Hello. It's Sally.'

'Good Lord, Sally! Where are you? How are you? Still living in the midlands? Just a minute, I'll turn the telly down...Sally! Now tell me everything. It's so long since I've heard from you.'

'Slow down! One question at a time...How's whatsname, Bill?'

'Oh he's buggered off, two months ago now. Couldn't take the pace. How's Graham?'

'Oh he's buggered off too!' Laughter. 'Though alas, only for two weeks. He's gone to Japan for some training thing or other. So tell me, are you all broken-hearted?'

'You mean about Bill going? Well...maybe a little. I suppose I was at first. Found out he was bonking some slut at the university...really Sal, like we used to say, they're All.'

'All. Every one.'

'Do you know, I was nearly faithful to him. Can you imagine that? Me *faithful*?'

'What do you mean *nearly* faithful? that's like saying *nearly* a virgin!'

'That's me darling, nearly a virgin. And what about you? Any deliciousness in the neighbourhood? I hear these Midland men have nothing else on their minds - largely, I suppose, because there's nothing else to do. Is it true? Have you been faithful? Nearly faithful? Virginal?'

'Nearly,' I said, laughing. 'Very, very nearly.'

'Well come on, give me the details!'

I couldn't. Not even to her. 'I will when I see you', I said.

'Come on Sal, don't be bashful with me. How many points?' This was a reference to the Man Grading System we used to operate at college.

'Many many,' I said.

'More than three? Come on.'

'I'll tell you when I see you.' I insisted.

'Hey,' she said on a sudden thought, 'have you heard the latest on Barbara and Chris?'

Mutual Friend Time. 'What?'

'Gone off to America, right in the sticks. He pulled some high-flying research job. Pompous ass...Makes you sick!'

'That type always makes it to the top. I wonder how their matching kagouls go down in redneck country.'

'A treat I'd bet!' she said, laughing, 'so when are you coming to Bristol?'

I took a deep sigh. 'Not for a while I think. I'm in hospital again, just for a little while...'

'Oh darling!' her voice brimmed with genuine concern. 'What's the matter? Is it worse?'

'Um, I don't know...' and a deep of sadness opened under me. I told her all the latest, how they said the

Lymphoma was growing, and about the two opposing prognoses, and what Cathy said, and everything. And while I was talking it felt so *good* to be sharing it with somebody, especially my dear old friend who I trust and should not have neglected...

I usually think of Tammy as a self-obsessed charmer, often too deep in her own shallowness to listen much to anybody else. But that's rather unfair, because she loves being at the centre of peoples' lives, which involves her in their troubles...that's unfair too. She has a genuine warm heart. 'Darling,' she said when I was all talked out, 'I'm so sorry. Do you want me to come and see you?'

'No, don't do that. You have your job and everything.'

'You need someone to look after you. How could that bastard Graham go off and leave you now? You must have someone who cares for you *there*.'

'Oh,' I said, feeling a sudden regret for having laid myself so open. 'I have a friend here, right here in the hospital...'

'Who? A man?'

'No no, a young girl. I should say a young woman. Don't come and see me. You know I hate a fuss.'

'I'll think about it,' she said, lightly threatening. 'Promise to 'phone me, often. Wait. Give me your number and I'll 'phone you too.'

We did that and then said goodbyes.

I think I'll sleep tonight, pills or no.

CHAPTER TWO

SATURDAY

I'm going to have to revise my opinions about this hospital. They came to take me for radiation first thing this morning, and I would have bet any money they don't work weekends...

*

George and Tom know about the cancer. They came to see me this afternoon. It didn't take much intelligence for them to realise that this section of the hospital is not devoted to Women's Problems.

They were very sweet, of course. My room is awash with flowers. When the window is open the warm sweet breath of summer wafts around my prison, a sultry and cloying presence. Unwelcome, taunting. I want to be in my garden. I think of the house now with a slight and sneaky - and shamed regret.

Anyway, I was telling you about George and Tom. I may like Tom after all. He has a wicked, clever subtle sense of humour and while his face shows sour his words are usually ticklish.

In fact he sometimes makes George seem rather dull and a little silly.

Liking Tom makes me feel a little guilty about the George episode. Or rather, it should! But as I write this, a big grin spreading unbidden over my face, I want to write 'Heee Heeee'. There, I did it.

It was kind of them to have come. Tom asked me frankly about the cancer and I told them some of the truth, keeping my language entirely objective as if I were talking about somebody else. I can do this with some people, detach myself from the whole process and observe it.

(I wish I could do this *all* the time! I'm *not* strong. I'm *no* heroine.)

(And there are times when I have these brief irresistible attacks of self-pity, my dark secret...I think this Counsellor person will be useful after all. I can say anything I like to her. If she ever comes to see me.)

What else did we talk about? I don't think we mentioned Mary Dyne more than once or twice (what is *happening* to my memory?). I told them she was still here (must 'phone her when I've finished this), they said good.
There's been little or no progress on the wendy-house. Joan and Harry are still in London buying equipment.

I was sorry when they left, even though they did make me miss a program I wanted to watch...what was it?

SUNDAY

Mary-Dyne came to see me last night! Or rather this morning, It must have been around 3am. I was sleeping the sleep of the drugged, very deep and delicious, when my subconscious registered that I couldn't breathe. Millions of years of survival training caused self-preservation circuits to cut in, forcing me awake to find a child's hand clamped over my mouth.

Luckily I was too drugged to be frightened. Besides, opening my eyes to find Mary-Dyne looking down at me with a finger to her lips reassured me quickly enough to prevent panic. Despite the microsecond's who-am-I-where-am-I and why reaction.

'Sally! Sally! Are you awake?'

I was overcome with relief, hugged her. 'What's happening? How did you get here?' I asked.

'I walked, how else? Snuck out of the ward like a ghost. The Night Sister is fast asleep, and there's no-one on guard here, as far as I can see.'

'The Duty Nurse is somewhere around, you can be sure of that. Close the door.'

She obeyed, and as she limped to the door dragging her plaster-encased leg I turned the bedside lamp on.

'See?' she said proudly, 'I can move about easily. No trouble.'

'As long as no-one sees you!'

'Gosh yes,' she giggled. 'Though it's not going to be easy to delay their throwing me out much longer. Besides, this leg itches like hell. Sometimes I'd do *anything* to rip off the plaster and give it a good scratch!'

'That means it's getting better. Come and sit down.'

'Sally,' Mary-Dyne said as she eased herself into the chair at the side of the bed, 'How much longer do I have to keep this up? When can I go home?'

I shrugged. 'I don't know dear. We're waiting for Joan and Harry to get back from London with all the equipment - '

'The bugs?' she asked excitedly.

'And things. You know we can't let you go home until we're all set up. You'll just have to be patient. George and Tom - they're part of the team - came to see me yesterday. They've almost finished the wendy-house, but -'

'The Observation Post!'

I laughed at the way she insists on translating the mundane into the mysterious. 'Yes,' I said, 'once the equipment arrives, all it will take is a lick of paint and it'll be ready.'

'It's all so terribly thrilling!...and,' she added, 'so good of all these people to take so much trouble for me!' She leaned forward and gave me a peck on the cheek.

'Don't bother being grateful,' I said. 'Obviously we all *need* this project, almost as much as you do.'

'In what way?'

'Oh they're all bored to death in their little Spiroid world. They should be grateful to *you*...'

She laughed gaily and then, realising the danger of being heard she clamped a hand on her mouth.

'Anyway,' she said, 'that's enough about me. How are they treating you?'

'Uh, oh, I'm fine you know, nothing serious - 'I couldn't (and still can't) remember if Mary-Dyne knows about the cancer or not. I waffled.

'Good!' she said, dismissing the subject; which made me feel a mixture of regret and relief. 'Well I'd better go now,' she said busily, 'we don't want them noticing my bed is empty. Keep me informed. 'Phone me lots.'

*

My third treatment, and it's *Sunday*. Sorry again Hospital for having doubted you. It's undignified, but I just have to stop being me and adapt to being an inanimate object that allows itself to be manipulated by experts...

And so here am I back again and I can feel boredom creeping into the room, like a fog that gets harder to see through...Sleep? Read? Pull bell? That new male nurse is rather good looking in a mawkish too-tall ginger way. I don't think we're going to be friends.

*

I am so tired but there's no way I can sleep. What an afternoon! To think I was *bored*...

The first thing that happened after lunch was George and Tom arriving. I had been trying to watch the television, and after only fifteen minutes of cartoons my neck was hurting already, and a major headache was building up.

Enter G & T (hee hee) preceded by flowers. Each simultaneously kissed the opposite sides of my forehead in greeting. The statutory 'How are you today?' fended off with the obligatory 'Much better.' A lie. Last night after M D left (M-D G&T tee hee) I couldn't sleep, lay there sweating and nauseous. Today I have a lot of pain in the lower back. And pain in the head. I could really do with a massage.

'That's good!' Tom said. 'Because, dear Sally, we've decided that this is an excellent place for a meeting.'

Oh no, I thought. 'Excellent,' I said. 'Here? When?'

'No don't joke,' George admonished me, 'Tom wants to see all the Foggies together, so how else could we do that?'

'Why, Tom? Why do you want to see everyone together?' I asked.

'Well, seeing as how that Colonel fellow - '

'Major,' George corrected.

'*Major* then, and his woman - '

'I hardly think Joan's his woman - ' I said, then stopped myself at the amazing thought that he could be right. 'Even if she is, does it matter?'

'Well....I *suppose* - ' Tom drew out this last word with camp mock-cynicism, 'there's nothing wrong with a bit of rumpy, even at their age...'

'What Tom's trying to say is he's sceptical.'

'About what?' I abandoned my attempts to sneak a look at the tv to find out how Captain Kracker would escape from the Dreaded Kreons, and flicked the thing off.

'Well for starters, where are they?' Tom asked.

'In London,' I said. Then, less confidently, 'I suppose...'

'That's what I told him,' George said. 'They've gone to buy the equipment.'

'Hm. That's their story...' Tom said archly. Then 'have you seen whatsname? Anniemary?'

'Seen her and talked to her,' I answered. 'She visited me in the dead of night.'

They laughed. 'What? Here? Secretly?' George asked.

'Yes,' I smiled, pulled the bedclothes toward me as they sat either side of the bed.

'What did she say?' Tom asked, and I told them how she was faking pain, doing anything to prolong her stay.

Just as I finished the story, people arrived. Margaret Meld entered like a thin impersonation of herself. She's one of those women who spends her life in public trying to make herself as small as possible.

I greeted her, and the couple who followed her in. They're called Bob and Caroline. These people are the sort who don't have a surname or if they do, it's the sort of name that dissolves in the mind like sherbet. 'Just call me Bob' and 'Just call me Caroline.' It must be hard going through life without anything remotely remarkable ever happening. And now they're faced with the opportunity of participating in a miniseries about child-killers and espionage...

Memory Test No 1: Can I remember what they look like? I seek them here I seek them there

Wait, it's coming. Bob is blond I think, or has light brown hair with a touch of the ginger. A gawky man with glasses, mostly smile. The 'Ladywife' (pause for bilious attack) is coiffeured fake blond, close to peroxide white. Red lips, no other facial features come to mind. Her role is to provide the giggles, and the earnest nods at whatever Hubby says. If she has any opinions, I'd bet they're his.

More people crowded in. First of the rest was McCarthy, who then took on the role of Major-Domo, prefacing each introduction with 'In the (Portnoy/Blandford/Cumbria) at number (whatever)...' before inviting them to 'Meet Mrs Alpert, whose has so kindly allowed us to use her garden...'

And to my embarrassment and delight, after each introduction Tom would lean forward and whisper wicked comments.

The other Foggies are (Memory Test Number 2:):

1: Russell and Joy Hoban (Tom: 'They're the ones with the *caravan* . The locals hate them.') Fat, jolly, middle-aged.

2: The Davies ('Used to be a charwoman. Married the boss...puts on such *airs* my dear')

3: Mavis and Willy Garthorn ('Local councillor. One child, precocious brat, keeps a horse in their garage...')

4: Patrick and Gordon - surnames? ('Gay couple of course. The blond, the older one - he's a schoolteacher and the boy's only nineteen. Ex-pupil. The *Estate* thinks they're brothers.')

5: Mr and Mrs Henry ('She runs all the Tupperware parties on the Estate. Represents Avon, double-glazing company, all sorts. *Desperate* for money.'

6: Mr Barton ('The one with the Rottweiler. Baaad news. Do Not Annoy.')

More and more! They kept crowding in! When the door was finally and officiously closed by the McCarthy, there were about 23 people crammed into my tiny cell. Some sat on the other bed, those who had arrived first were all over the four chairs, others stood about uncomfortably.

'I'm going to call this meeting to order now,' McCarthy announced. Minutes of previous meeting? Ah yes. All subscriptions are now paid, so that item lapses. Any comments? No? I'll proceed then.' She stopped and glared around the room. 'Any objections to my taking the chair?'

('If she can find one!' Tom tittered in my ear.)

'Agenda items,' McCarthy said. 'You called this Extraordinary Meeting Mr Champion. What do you want to discuss?'

'I want this meeting to discuss the absence of our leaders,' Tom said.

'Ah yes, I forgot. Apologies.' She consulted her notebook. 'Apologies from Major Frost and Mrs Bellings who have urgent business in the Capital.'

'You've had apologies from them?' Tom asked wonderingly.

'Indeed. I had a telephone call - '

'When?' Tom asked.

'Oh, uh - ' looking down at her book, 'Thursday. Yes, the fifteenth. Ms Bellings said that if we were to call a meeting in their absence we should accept their apologies.'

'That's *your* theory down the tubes,' George smirked.

'Then why have they been away so long?' Tom asked defensively.

'It takes a while to organise these things.' McCarthy said patronisingly, 'Besides, they haven't even been gone a

142

week yet. You can be sure that whatever reason they have, they are working on our behalf.'

'Please - ' I said, feeling suddenly claustrophobic, 'could somebody open a window?' I drew my legs up under the covers and hugged my knees, wondering if I was going to be sick. Two of my visitors took this as an invitation to join George and Tom on my bed.

'We're all putting a great deal of money into this project,' a fat woman with big hoop earrings said, 'I think we need to know what's being done with it...'

'Surely you're not suggesting that the major is in any way - unreliable?' McCarthy asked aggressively.

'*Sergeant* major, ' Tom said.

'Charming man', somebody with a high voice said.

'That Mrs Bellings is the right sort of Englishwoman,' A gruff, snarling voice commented. 'Unlike some of these immigrant chappies - '

By now I was gasping for air. 'Please,' I said piteously, '*Somebody* open the window...'

'I think there's something fishy going on - '

'The Major showed me how to prune roses - '

'He's a gentleman - '

'Order, order!'

'This is all a waste of time. Everything is going to plan - '

'Please, please - the *window* - !'

'Nobody has even *mentioned* whats'name, Mary Ann - !' Tom erupted, really angry.

'Tom, just a minute, Sally - ' this was George's voice, and it was almost the last thing I heard before passing out...and as the room faded I could hear the door opening and the raised, incredulous voice of Sister ordering *everyone out right away!* This is not a place for Poblic Meeting!...

MONDAY

Monday morning. It's very quiet in a busy-hospital kind of way. Sister has promised not to let in any visitors. 'You got to be relaxed for your treatment,' she said, 'I don't know what Doctor will say when she hear about the shenanigan yesterday...'

Ring...that was Mary Dyne to say hello. 'Isn't it boring,' she said. 'I do hate Monday mornings. How are you?'

'Feeling much better', I answered automatically.

'I have to get out of here,' Mary-Dyne said with a sigh. 'There's just nothing to do...'

I was tempted to tell her about the meeting yesterday, but had second thoughts. 'No dear, not yet. We haven't got the equipment we need. It'll be any day now...How much longer can you keep it up?'

'Ooh, not long. They're doing x-rays and scans and things tomorrow, and they're being very annoying. They think I'm imagining the pain. I find this insulting. I've always considered myself rather a good actress...'

'And as soon as they find out there's nothing seriously wrong - '

'I'll be out!'

'Hm. I suppose we *could* give it a quick whack with a sledgehammer...'

She laughed. 'I've thought of that. I have no idea where I could get one here...' her tone changed suddenly, went formal. 'Thank you for 'phoning Marigold, but I have to go now. My mother's come to visit.'

'Find a way to delay! Remember!' I said.

'Yes I will, I promise,' she said brightly. 'Well, 'bye now.'

*

Damn 'phone. I shouldn't have one. Suddenly everybody wants to talk to me. Graham, to reassure himself that he doesn't have to rush back; Tom, to ask if I have recovered from yesterday - with effusive apologies, feeling so guilty etc etc. Tammy, to find out how I am. There seems little to say to her. I prefer lying to receiving sympathy...

I feel as if some people resent my illness, as a dreadful inconvenience to them. Others - like Tammy, as a delightfully exciting addition to her life - is that fair? Mary-Dyne sees it as an irrelevance, a convenience designed especially to give her some companionship in hospital.

My task is to reassure everybody, make them feel good and virtuous...this isn't fair on me.

CHAPTER THREE

TUESDAY

A medical conference at my request in my room. All three of my doctors together at one time. I'm sure this is unheard of, a first.

But I achieved this: I now understand much less about what is happening to my body and have no idea about the effectiveness of my treatment.

'This radiation we're giving you is something new,' Dr Patel said, 'Short bursts to the infected areas, very intensive. We hope this way to achieve more in the short-term you see.'

'Will it help with the headaches?' I asked.

'Probably,' he smiled. 'Those swellings on the neck are the most likely cause of your headaches, restricting the blood supply to the brain. This would also explain the nausea.'

'And the sweating at night?' I asked. I'm always sweating, though it's worst at night. My temperature goes up and down between 99 and 100. If they can relieve the symptoms just a little bit...I began to feel reassured.

Monster soon put paid to that. 'And then we'll try the chemotherapy,' he said.

'If it's necessary!' Patel said sharply. They were obviously continuing an argument.

'Come now Patel, anybody with the experience I have in Oncology could tell you - '

'I don't wish to discuss this now!' Patel frowned him a warning.

'Now is a good time. This Mrs - uh - patient - is far too advanced - '

'Please Dr Maister!' Patel took in the dismay on my face, and was becoming angry. 'This is not the time...'

'Well, it's *time* that will tell!' Maister said smugly. 'I'm always right about these matters, you should know that by now...'

'Right are you? *Right*, eh? Do you remember Barrows? Eh? You said he wouldn't last six months...'

'Ah, that was an exceptional case. Divine intervention, I suspect...'

'WHAT? That was purely medical intervention I assure you...besides, as I said this is not the place. I suspect we should carry on this discussion outside, what do you say?'

'Outside is it?' Maister said with what I can only describe as an evil grin. 'If that's the way you want it!'

'Good!'

'Good!'

And the two consultants made dramatic exits, hospital gowns flapping behind them like cloaks.

It took Cathy nearly half an hour to calm me down and for me to realise that the only way to get her to leave would be to pretend to have been reassured...

(I do like Dr Patel, the way he shrugs off all my anxieties, promises his ideas will work. He's so *sure*! The sort of man you could use to prop up a falling house. Which is, after all, his job.)

(I wonder if I should ask for an HIV test.)

(What for?)

CHAPTER FOUR

THURSDAY

Hello dear Journal. I'm sorry I haven't been in contact with you for two - or is it three? - days, what a long time, what a little has happened. I had my scan this morning. They put me into this shiny white tube, a high-tech womb which invades me with invisible rays, no sensation at all except cold...they'll give me the results 'later'. I wonder when 'later' is.

Daily radiation, and, strange to relate, I do feel a little better. I'm sleeping more, I don't seem to be sweating as much, though I notice that my bedclothes always seem to stink in the morning, despite the fact that they change the sheets daily. Mary-Dyne and I have been having a telephone conversation once or twice a day. We're becoming very close. I feel like her older sister and dear friend. She depends on me; our conversations usually consist of her chattering away for, say, four fifths of the time and my using the remaining fifth to reassure her that I love her (she demands this), that I'll protect her and believe in her.

This sometimes feels like an onerous responsibility; she has fitted me into a role I'm not so sure that I can fulfil. Well, I can understand her need for a mother/sister figure, the 'best friend' of all the schoolgirl books. She has never had anyone with whom she can talk intimately, someone who values her, trusts her and more important, *values* her.

If I die soon - and I don't think I will, by the way - she'd have the ground whipped from beneath. She's fall a long way.

I have to admit that she fulfils a great need for me as well. I need a Best Friend...she's neither mature enough nor wise enough to take this role but where Tammy fails (I speak to her daily too) Mary-Dyne fills in. (At least Tammy listens to *me* some of the time.) With Tammy I can say just how I'm feeling, the latest on treatment - strangely this doesn't bore her as much as I would have thought. I can talk about sex, though I still haven't told her about George! - I can talk about how Graham stifles me, how I hate his gilded cage...all these things. So I get love and sympathy from Tammy and give it to Mary-Dyne.

...And so betwixt the two of them, I lick my platter clean...

*

Tammy has become obsessed by my cancer. The absence of a man in her life is to blame for this. She is basically an obsessive personality and when she grabs an idea between her teeth she becomes a British Rottweiler.

She has been to libraries, phoned medicals she knows, (including Chris and Barbara who are doing research in Cancer in the American West somewhere) spoken to everyone about everything. She has become almost as much an expert as I am. She continually interrogates me about my symptoms and treatment. Large proportions of our conversations consist of her asking 'Have you/they tried/ heard of...' She has sent me articles hailing New Alternative treatments by the score. (The one on my lap now next to the Journal is by a Dr Eleni Pappadopoulis of Perth Australia, about how if I take massive doses of vitamin C I'll detoxicate myself.)

She nags me about this place in Bristol which specialises in alternative treatments. She has no faith in my doctors, which annoys me. Though to be honest, my faith in them isn't of too high an order. I seem to have become something of a medical football, kicked between Maister and Patel. I often feel that the Monster wants me to die, just to prove his point.

Yet I have to respect him as an Oncologist; he has a high success rate, which he has told me a dozen times. He tries to be charming sometimes, which is strange.

Patel can be unctuous, irritating. He is also patronising, yet what he says is usually sensible. He is a ridiculous poseur; he poses, as if for the front cover of an adult sex magazine, one hand twitching away stray locks from his forehead, thrusting his thigh out coquettishly as he says, 'Don't you worry Mrs. You're in the best of hands.'

FRIDAY

I've had the results of the scan. Cathy has just left. She says lungs heart and spleen are now showing traces of the disease. And I thought I was feeling better! She says she's spoken to the Marsden in London and they can admit me within a month. She wants me out of the clutches of the Doctor Wars.

Apparently this is how it works: I am in the Advanced Stage of the disease, and the best treatment (whatever Patel says...the monster was right) is combination chemotherapy. This treatment is successful in 70 - 90% of cases, though about a third of patients have relapses and have to be treated again. These patients - apart from 15 or so percent - die.

Cathy showed me a colour picture of the cancerous cells, the bastard invaders. Dammit haven't they a right to thrive too? Yet by thriving they destroy their host, like voracious humans destroying their planet. They'll die from their greed, if they're not killed off by a miracle first. Serves the little bastards right. Cathy explains things so well, I'm very lucky to have her as my physician.

Here's how she explained chemotherapy: It's like a fire brigade going into a burning house with axes. Much is demolished in order to put out the blaze. The difference, luckily, is that the human body can regenerate itself. Things grow back again, eventually. 'We may well do some damage,' she said, 'but the chances are we'll put out the fire.'

Chances are.

*

Another letter from Tammy, with a photocopied article from the Omaha World Record. More - I'll just read the letter - 'I had this from Barbara this morning and had to send it to you right away. Did I tell you she and Chris went off to Omaha to do research into cancer? Omaha *Nebraska* would you believe. Anyway, I have always been vague about what Christopher is doing out there, and I telephoned her the other day to tell her about you and find out. Sadly, Chris' research is to do with Leukaemia, not Lymphoma, but it's all much the same thing isn't it? And they're nearing a breakthrough using something called Antisense - she claims it will be the same sort of revolution in cancer treatment as antibiotics have been for infections. Isn't that exciting! I told her all about your case and she faxed me this, which I send you with hope and love...'

The Omaha World Herald article is headed 'MAN MADE GENETIC DRUG USED IN PIONEERING CANCER TREATMENT' ...It's very sweet and kind of Tammy but I have now read so many articles I'm sick to death of them. Ooh, Freudian pun. anyway these things take *years* to get onto the market. The Americans have to test them every which way, and the drug companies have to ensure that their profits are in millions. Or billions? It says here that they are trying it on their first patient...he looks so Alternative. He's wearing a headscarf - is this because chemo has removed his hair? He has earrings... a sweet face. I send him love, from my bed to his. Don't die, sweet-faced boy.

*

He died. Tammy has just plunged me into the depths again by telling me oh so casually, 'Oh that doesn't prove anything! They were only doing toxicity tests, very low dosage. But the exciting thing is I spoke to Chris last night, he says it's all looking very good indeed - '

'He died,' I said. The article was on my table and I picked it up and looked into that face again and tears -

'That's not the point at all! The thing is, it wasn't the treatment that killed him - '

'He died!'

'Will you stop *saying* that! It doesn't matter! It's only the beginning of the game...'

My patience ran out. 'He died, ' I said, and put the 'phone down.

*

I feel guilty because she's such a good friend and her love for me is absolutely genuine. But I'm angry too because she just doesn't realise how *futile!* - it is! - to feed me dreams and hopes and *useless!* - information about things which *may!* - or may not - have any relevance to me because they will all be too late too ...

*

I felt so guilty I telephoned her and said so and we had a tearful reconciliation and I now have to pay for it. She's coming up. I tried to dissuade her, the last thing I want is sad-eyed friends trying to cheer me up. No good! She will stay at my house (she's never seen it before, poor thing, what a shock -) (THAT'S why I never invited her to visit! After all!) But that's tough she can think what she likes...maybe I'm happy she's coming. I must ask myself. It'll only be for the weekend. I will be cheery, I will act happy, I must summon strength for this...we the dying – upon whom the onus rests for reassuring those who love us...

SATURDAY

They've just left. George, Tom, Tammy...and Mary-Dyne! She has a walking-cast, they've x-rayed her and they're discharging her on Monday. This is fine, I'll be home Tuesday - at least that was the original plan - Cathy seemed a little unsure when I asked her. But I think it will be o.k. for me to be at home until a bed is available at the Marsden.

I don't know what Mary-Dyne will do.

I have to tell you what happened, before I turn on the telly and try to forget everything: Because everything's now upside-down and so am I...: REVELATION:

It was 2pm or so when Tammy arrived. We did all the greetings and catchings up and how-are you-s and then George burst in, all breathless excitement.

I introduced them, but George was more interested in telling me: 'WHAT a kerfuffle! You'll never guess what's happened!' he planted a too-sweet kiss on my cheek and sat on the opposite side of the bed to Tammy.

'No I wouldn't. Tell.'

'That Harry - and his concubine I suppose, Joan - have conned us. All!'

'But - good heavens! That means - '

'Tom was right!' George finished my sentence.

'Well, tell me how you found out,' I begged.

'Are you lying comfortably? Then I'll begin...this morning Tom 'phoned me from work. He had to go up to the New Town to get some supplies or something. Anyway, while he's there he checks Estate Agent windows as always, making sure his investment hasn't gone down too much, and what does he see?'

George waited like a good mother for me to say 'What?'

'A picture of a house on the estate, with a "Sold" sticker.'

'So?' I said, not understanding.

'Number 23!' he said, 'Major Frosts's house!'

Well, you can imagine what I was thinking. 'What do you mean it's sold?' I asked.

'Sold! Gone! And I'd like to bet the same has happened to that Bellings woman's!' - conveniently forgetting how buddy-buddy he had been with Joan. 'Tom knew - or suspected at any rate - that there was something funny going on, though he didn't know exactly what. But this confirms it. If they've sold their houses, they've run off with all our money...'

'And are somewhere in South America spending it right now!' I couldn't suppress the rising of a grin.

George was smiling now, too. 'Can you imagine! - ' he said, 'The Bonny and Clyde of Suburbia!'

'Conned the whole neighbourhood! The Granny and Grampa Gang!'

By now the grins had turned to titters and the titters were growing into belly-laughs.

'All those meetings! All the spy stuff! What on earth is Fatty McCarthy going to say!'

We were roaring with laughter and it was some time before Tammy managed to interpolate - 'Would somebody please let me in on the joke?'

We calmed down enough to give her a précis of the Mary-Dyne saga, and when she had heard the story she, too, began to laugh.

'A *brilliant* scam! Pure blackmail!'

'*Easily* worth a thousand pounds!'

We were completely overcome with laughter, were making such a noise that Sister poked her head in anxiously, shook it, and took it away again.

It was lovely to laugh...and George looked so lovely laughing.

...and after some more of that sort of thing I demanded details. 'So then what happened? Has Tom gone to the Police?'

'Well no, he wants to call a Meeting first...'

The idea of another pompous formal meeting, and the reactions of the others made us laugh again.

'Anyway,' he continued, 'Tom did some 'phoning around of all the estate agents in the town until he found the one that sold the Bellings mansion, so it's confirmed. They've definitely decamped.'

'Phew!' Tammy said, 'it's a great story. How much do you reckon they made?'

'Well,' George said, there were twenty three households involved...'

'Which means they got twenty thousand pounds,' I explained.

'More!' George said. 'I know for a fact that McCarthy gave two...'

'It's not a massive amount of money is it?' Tammy said. 'I mean, say thirty five or so - not enough to run away to Brazil with, surely?'

'Oh I don't know,' George said, 'Add that to the two hundred thousand or so from their houses, makes a nice sum with which to retire to the Third World. They've probably been planning it for years. That letter the newsagent showed you - that must have been a fake!'

'It's unbelievable...' I said.

*

I think it was on the word 'unbelievable' that Mary-Dyne pushed the door open and entered the room.

Somewhere 'round there anyway.

We all reacted as if caught by mommy playing doctors and nurses.

We had forgotten all about Mary-Dyne! I certainly had - I've just reviewed the last few pages, and that's proof. How could we have just - I feel so guilty as I write this. Go on.

'Hello,' she said, and then she saw the confusion on our faces and asked immediately, 'What's the matter? I thought you'd be happy to see me - '

'I am, I am! Come in, dear' I was feeling thoroughly fake and my invitation must have sounded insincere because she entered diffidently, with suspicious glances at my guests.

I introduced Tammy to her. George she knows already.

Conversation flagged. 'So they let you out, then?' I asked.

'Yes. This is my new cast. They wanted me to walk to try it out...so I came to visit.'

'Well you're very welcome,' I said.

There was a pause as Mary-Dyne looked around the room suspiciously. 'What's the matter?', she asked.

There was no avoiding it. I told her.

She listened in numbed silence.

Then, eyes brimming with tears, she stumped out of the room.

*

After she left and we had an earnest discussion about what to do.

'I'm going to tell the police everything,' George said at last. 'Whatever the Foggies decide.'

'That sounds about right,' Tammy said, 'I don't know why you didn't think of that before.'

'We did, we certainly did,' I said, 'Harry and Joan thought it would be useless...'

'They would!' George remarked grimly. 'We'll have to tell them everything. The whole foolish Foggy thing...'

'We're going to look stupid,' I said, 'Very, very stupid.'

'And we'll still be left with the primary problem...'

'Yes. The little girl in danger.'

We were interrupted by Nurse Simmons, who poked her head in to offer me my evening tablets and a cup of tea. 'You all right dear?' she asked solicitously. She had obviously been warned by Sister to protect me from strangers.

'Fine,' I said.

'You sure now? Maybe it's time for visitors to leave. It is nine o'clock.' She nodded meaningfully in the direction of my visitors.

'I get the message,' George said, 'Look, don't worry about anything Sally. Just concentrate on getting better. I promise you we'll work out something to do.'

'Let me know what happens,' I said as Tammy, too, took her leave.

'Just don't worry.' He gave me a thoughtful, brief peck on the cheek, which was followed by another from Tammy. Then they left together.

*

"Don't worry. Don't worry"! How the hell can I not worry?

Dear Journal, listen: It's midnight now and I'm wide awake and I think I'm going crazy. I can't think straight. (These sleeping pills don't work. All they do is make me muzzy and muggy and unable to think.) If the cancer don't kill me the worry will. Not the first woman to worry herself to death I suppose. I can't stop thinking about Mary-Dyne, that innocent, desperate little girl lying up there in the Children's' Ward trusting us all. For her this is all the Big Adventure, which is bound to end up with Good Triumphing over Evil.

Because, she thinks, all these clever adults are on her side, working for her.

And what happens? The stupid greed of small people! The propensity of some people to see any situation as an opportunity to feather nests and fulfil empty dreams...I can just imagine what Spireslea will do when it hears about this. They'll panic about their lost money, that's all they'll be concerned about. The pips will squeak! And no-one will give a thought for the girl.

I can see the tabloid headlines now: SWINDLE IN SUBURBIA - *bogus Major runs away with neighbours' savings*... and the Tweeds will be off like bullets from a gun, set themselves up somewhere else and when the time is right Mary will fall under a bus or...

CHAPTER FIVE

ALONE AT LAST!! No chance of sleeping now, that's for sure. There are only three hours before we catch the plane and we're going to have to sneak out of the house before daylight, just to make sure.

This gives me about an hour to write down what happened, to pack, to lock up the house...this is so exciting! I feel like a naughty child about to go on holiday!

Right, write: The past few hours have been mad, mad. It started at 3am, when this bell woke me. I had finally dropped off despite my busy mind, and the endless thrumming riiiing broke right into my drugged sleep.

Feeling as if there was a thick puffy cloud in my head I lay there for a while wondering what was happening. Feet, plenty of feet flapped past the door and eventually I realised that the ringing must have some meaning, some specific meaning. Something like - Fire?

The word shook me like a wake-up call and I dragged myself out of the bed, to the door.

I looked out into the corridor. A male nurse (the ginger one, I forget his name) rounded the corner, came running toward me. 'What's happening?' I asked.

Irritated by the question, he forced himself to stop. He was panting. 'Nothing,' he said. 'Go back to bed.'

'What's the bell? Fire?' I asked.

'Yes', he snapped. 'Go back to bed.'

Fire terrifies me ...when I was a child, the parents took us for a holiday at St Ives in Cornwall. Half the town burned down one night. I watched all the panic and terror. I saw how cruelly fire eats things. 'How the hell can I go back to bed?' I sputtered, 'It's a fire!'

'For God's sake woman, get back to your room and close the door! It's a fire!' There was panic in his eyes now.

It spread itself to me. 'I have to get out!' I cried.

'Calm down!' he said, 'Everything will be all right!', and with this he ran off down the passage.

I had to get out. I remember thinking, what does one *take*? And what I grabbed was: This Journal, my toiletries and my handbag.

Shaking and sweating, I left my flower-bower to burn, dashed down the corridor, almost fell down the stairs (I remembered not to use the lift in case the power cut out) and found myself in Reception. A woman shaped like a large pudding sat at the desk, looked up with a quizzical smile. 'Where are you off to dear?', she asked with a smile.

'It's a fire!' I blurted. 'We have to get out! Evacuate the hospital!'

'Don't be silly, dear,' she said, 'go back to bed. It's only those workers upstairs.'

'On a Saturday night?! - it's fire!' I said, unable to accept her bland reassurances.

She frowned as if trying to understand. 'A fire you say?'

'Yes! Can't you hear the bell?'

She cupped a podgy hand to an ear. 'Something *is* ringing,' she admitted.

'It's a *fire* bell, you stupid creature!'

'I see,' she said, with a sigh. 'I suppose I'd better call 999.'

'Good idea,' I said, and sat on the chair by her window as she followed her own advice.

Then there was chaos. All of a sudden it was as if all the extras from a B-movie had arrived at once; people dressed as patients, people undressed, people dressed as medics, nurses, ancillaries filled the lobby in a chatting, nervous throng.

'Isn't it exciting!' Mary-Dyne said, as she pushed her way through some extras and hopped over to me.

'Exciting? It's frightening!' I said.

'Oh no, not at all,' she said like a teacher correcting a foolish pupil. 'Nobody will be hurt, it's only a little fire, and we're safe aren't we?'

This sounded perfectly reasonable to me. I took a deep breath. It smelled of smoke.

'Everybody stay calm,' a man in a white coat standing on a chair said. 'If we're all calm everything will soon be under control.'

The low frightened murmurs of the crowd quietened a little. It felt good to have someone taking control. 'If we can organise Team B now,' he said, 'Evacuate the bed-bound, Team A will escort everybody here into the car park, Team C - '

Two things happened at once. A large, angry puff of smoke erupted into the lobby from the stair-well; and the Fire Brigade swarmed in at the front door.

Chaos! Catastrophe! Caught between the smoke and the blocked doorway, patients, doctors, nurses, everybody panicked at once.

Screams!

That instant is a few frames of living video in my head. Whenever it replays I feel again those terrifying few seconds when reason fled from the minds of hundreds of people at once...and left blind mania behind...

The only person who held on to her reason as tightly as she held my arm, was Mary-Dyne.

Fortunately, we were near the door. Luckily, the fire-fighters stood aside for this wild crutch-yielding mad child, who was shouting, 'Out of the way, get out, fuck off! Out of the way!' as she dragged me through them and out into the night air.

'Where are we going?' I asked, taking in deep clean cold breaths.

'Home!' she said, laughing. 'Call me a cab!'

Automatic circuit cut in. 'You're a cab!' I said.

*

We reached my house at 4.00 am. It was a dank, misty, pre-dawn August morning, heavy with suspended raindrops. I let us in silently and we tiptoed upstairs where Tammy slept - in my bed - with George, his downy-haired arm draped heavily over her shoulder...

My instantaneous reaction was to turn and run; but we must have made a sound (perhaps Mary-Dyne emitted an involuntary 'Oh!', because Tammy stirred, opened eyes, saw us, registered what was happening, put a finger to her lips and mouthed, with one of those cat-got-the-cream smiles, 'SHUSH'.

I can't explain or define what I felt then. Clichés about Best Fried/Lover come to mind, but...after all...How! Could!...it was as if Tammy had pushed herself into my most secret place, stolen my treasure and run off...

Mary-Dyne broke the atmosphere by giggling through a hand clasped to her mouth...and George raised his beautiful head. He looked adorable, all tousled like that, black hair everyway, sleep still clinging like warm fog around his head.

When he saw me and Mary-Dyne standing at the side of the bed his mouth broke into a massive warm welcoming smile, entirely genuinely happy. 'My God,' he said, 'Sally, you're back!'

'They let you out? Have they finished your treatment?' Tammy asked, sitting up and holding the sheet to her shoulders modestly, so that only one insulting nipple poked out like a tongue.

'At this time of the morning?' I asked sarcastically. I was looking for some way to hurt her. 'No.' Then I added casually, 'The place burnt down.'

'What!' George said. 'You're not serious!'

'She is!' Mary-Dyne said triumphantly. 'We discharged ourselves! I torched the rad suite and we left...'

Now I had to sit down. I could scarcely breathe. The flounced pink armchair appeared beneath me. 'You - ' I managed to say, 'You - *you* - ! - Set fire - ! - '

'Of course! What else could I do?

'Wait a minute. Wait a minute! Are you saying you "torched" the hospital?' George was wide-awake, wide-eyed, incredulous.

'Only the Rad Suite. Nothing major. They'll soon put it out,' the child said defensively.

'But that's terrible!', Tammy said, 'People could be killed!'

'I had to get out, don't you see? I had to run away! If I hadn't done it, I'd have had to go home! Back to those murderers! I'd rather die...now I'll only have to go to prison, see? Somewhere safe...' She buried head in hands, sobbing deeply.

My heart broke. Everything in the world had fallen apart at once, and the only person who felt much the same was Mary-Dyne, and I hope you're going to understand this; you see, I've lost Graham, I've lost George now, even the dream of him...and my life too, probably, and now Mary-Dyne is all I have left...

If I had to write my own Report now it would read: Understanding, U; Hope, U; Future, U.

U for Useless.

Which is all the reason I put my arms around Mary-Dyne and hugged her and promised to protect her for ever, whatever the consequences...

'We'll go away, ' I promised, 'We'll go away together, somewhere safe, far away,' as we sobbed together.

'And I'll be with you' Tammy said, and her naked body was pushing itself up against us, her naked arm around my shoulders...'Don't you worry my darlings, I will help you...'

George attached himself too, naked, sweet, warm, dried sweat, and Tammy naked, sweet, white, glowing, we're a post-coital sandwich, hustled eventually into my own bed which is rich with last night's now dried exultations...fussed into some sort of frustrated pretend-calm...

Tammy and George getting dressed either side of the bed. I cannot talk. There is a weight on my chest, my lungs are squeezed. Mary-Dyne draped over the bedside chair, looking like a deflated Puck...for a just an instant they all looked rather menacing, frightening. I tried some deep, long breaths, a technique the Counsellor showed me. And gradually I began to calm down.

'What are we going to do now?' I asked, when I felt ready to speak. 'The Tweed will hear about the fire pretty soon. She'll be out looking for Mary-Dyne...'

'She'll be celebrating my death, you mean!' Mary-Dyne looked up just long enough to say.

'She'll probably be worried sick,' George said in a parentish voice. 'Besides, you're not recovered and you need looking after...'

'In prison!' she muttered.

'You're not going to prison, I told you, you're not going to prison,' I said.

'I can't go home! I can't *ever* go home! Even if the spy-things are in place...' she cried.

'No,' I said, raising myself on an elbow, 'she can't go home.'

'And the so-called Spy things are well out of the window...' George said sadly.

'But that means there's nothing...' she said, 'Nothing...'

'She's right,' I said, 'there's nothing at home for her. We'll have to go away somewhere.'

They all turned to me.

'Go away?' George echoed, the thought taking hold.

'Hey, I have a great idea!' Tammy said suddenly. 'Listen to me. I have one little word for you: OMAHA.'

'Omaha?'

BOOK III

CHAPTER ONE

The whirr-zizz of humming lawnmowers, the gentle swish of perfectly-controlled mechanical rain... I am, or appear to be, the only life there is in this Sleepy Hollow suburb of Omaha Nebraska. It's noon, and except for the mechanicals the place is deserted. Like a move set, waiting for action. Any moment a security guard will come to shoo me off.

The sun is stunning, soporific, cruel. There are clouds - and when they interpose themselves between me and the sun everything goes cool, very quickly.

Let me describe.

I'm lying on a lounger in a trimmed, tamed garden which has few flowers - Chris and Barbara haven't been in this rented house long (about five weeks I think) and haven't had time to plant anything new.

The garden itself is about fifty foot by fifty foot. Square. The grass is two inches long and I suspect it harbours vicious dangerous and strange foreign creatures, red of fang and antenna.

The house is built of orange brick. I'm told it dates from the twenties although it looks fifties. The peaked roof is an asbestos-topped pyramid, with balconies on the first floor either side. The wooden railings are broken and look like death-traps planted for careless guests. The house has fourteen cracked windows; apparently the previous tenants enjoyed throwing crockery at each-other. Chris tells me that the owner of the house promised to get everything fixed 'pretty soon'. He has adopted a mid-Atlantic accent, just enough to make inhabitants of either side of the water regard him as a foreigner.

The rooms are spacious, beautifully proportioned. A high, pointed arch separates the living-room from the study on the ground floor. The kitchen is a nightmare of orange Formica and fake wood, the lino cracked and ripped.

There is a vast cellar; rooms of it, containing the 'utilities' - which consists of a fiercely efficient, ancient washing-machine and dryer. Also two humming whirring boxes which, I'm told, are dehumidifiers without which the whole pile would turn into mould. There is also a central-heating boiler, a massive machine which looks as if, in say Harry Harryhausen's hands, it could turn instantaneously into a slavering monster determined to destroy the world.

There are three bedrooms upstairs, one for Chris and Barbara, one for Mary-Dyne, and the last for me. They are all sparsely furnished; I am sleeping on a brashly flowered IKEA sofa-bed. Mary-Dyne sleeps on a foldaway. Our host and hostess sleep on the biggest bed I have ever seen, it could house a whole Somali family easily.

Mary-Dyne is walking in the park. I don't know why. Walking nowhere, for nothing, seems rather futile to me. At least golf puts a purpose into walking; though it seems a silly game...

This American version of the Spireselea experience has some notable differences with the UK version. Firstly, each house is different here; there are a variety of styles, each a pastiche of an older one. There is fake American Colonial, with pillars and Adam-style porches; pastiche Tudor, beamed, pseudo-half-timbered fronts and fake leaded windows. Bogus parodies of Victorian Gothic, with towers and turrets and castellation. All the houses are fake *something,* as if there has never been an American architect with a single original thought. Even the few Modernist monstrosities, which nod in the direction of Frank Lloyd Wright, have the look of a stereotype or ideal of the modern, rather than a genuine original.

I suppose there must be a reason for this. I mean, each different but none original: I think it says something about American nouveau-bourgeois conservatism, allied with American Dream. The need for solidity and permanence, for the smug reassurance that whatever happens - hurricanes, marauding Indians, termites, economic collapse - roots are firmly planted where nothing ever happens, and nothing ever changes - Europe.

*

Resolution: stay grateful, happy, charming. Resolution: don't knock it. Chris and Barbara seem so happy, entwined around each-other and their work. (Barbara is Chris' technician, she's the one that peers through microscopes at the cancer cells she's growing, nurturing, loving - so that Chris can work out new ways to kill them.)

(That was how he met her. She was tamed by this vast hulking man when they were both working at the Royal Free in Bristol. I have to report - please, Fate, never let them get their hands on this Journal! - they look much like Laurel and Hardy. He the Looming Presence, tall, wide and hairy; she the tiny petite demure companion, fluttery-eyed in love with every burp and fart he makes. I never thought I would see her conquered!...

WATCH OUT! Here comes Nostalgia... We were a trio of terrors we were, me Tammy and Barbara back in them College days. Well, to men at least. We haunted the few clubs and bars of Bristol like homing harridans, having decided that the University facilities were far too full of pimply arrogant pseudo-intellectuals, thin men with rat-frantic minds, bed-to-bed leapfroggers, thigh-led egomaniacs...hang on, have I just described all men? *Surely* not...

Change gear. Mustn't get back onto *that* boring subject! Just a word or two more, then I'll go on...as I was saying, egomaniacs convinced that women are only waiting to be rescued from the bleak prison of virginity by their Holy Cock and therefore they were to be divided into two types, Yes and No. And the Yes Girls (the ones with the Acceptable Assets, who could be persuaded -), were they worth it anyway? Oh hell, have another pint.

I don't like my cynicism. But that is the way we used to think in those days. And we decided that if *that* was what they were like, we'd be *worse*! Turn the tables. Hunt them.

Purely as sex-objects.

And so we did what they do; we graded men on a scale, giving points out of ten for aspects of their appearance from the top of their heads to the tips of their toes. With an entire grading system for the penis of course.

Another system applied to the Actual Performance...

Oh yes! And the Points System for the pick-up; One point for Eyes Meeting, one for a Smile, one for chat-up, another for Invitation and the remaining six for Realisation...

You won't be very surprised when I tell you that we hardly ever left one of these dens with an Actual Man. We spent so much time evaluating and totting up points that we seldom had any left for a man to approach and say Hi. We used to put this down to what we referred to as the Peer Effect; the theory that each of us felt too self-conscious in the presence of the others to make any move for a man who didn't rate at least 8 out of 10.

Had we been on our own, no doubt we would have had plenty! I've seen many a six I could have been quite content to have spent a few steamy hours with...(Graham, by the way, is a five. George - damn him! - is a nine. The highest I've had, I reckon...)

*

Stopped for a moment to fume about George, make a cool drink. (How could he!/They; How dare he/they; That sort of stuff. I shouldn't be so annoyed, I have no rights over him. So why do I feel betrayed?)

I'm back now.

Thinking about it, I suppose that the truth is that most men would be far too intimidated to approach three girls together, especially when they look so predatory, so cynical and armoured, so critical and unfriendly. And the - sorry, 'phone ringing -

.......it went prrrrrrr,... prrrrrrr, just like in the movies! Such a gentle, subtly intrusive tone which says 'excuse me, I hate to bother you but.' Unlike the British Hey There! Hey there! Get up! Now!

It was Barbara to invite us to lunch with her. She will pick us up at twelve. I hope Mary-Dyne is back from her walk by then.

I have to tell a you little more about Bristol. (Freeeeze the past!) There was one thrilling embarrassing and almost catastrophic occasion when all three of us yes, I said all three! - went home with a married man called Barry, yes he who became my four-year lover, the same Barry who introduced me to Graham.

171

I hated that night. And Barry realised it, which was why we met again and talked and he said he was so ashamed about the whole business, invited everybody home because too shy to ask me, the one he really wanted...O how flattering...Water under bridge. Tears before bedtime. First Real Love. First experience of that Space invader, that Time-Consumer, that life-threatening horror show...(Did I say that he was Deputy Head at the School where I had my first - and only job? Coincidence? *Not at all.*)

*

Mary-Dyne arrived just as I finished writing the above, which was perfect. I'm now in my room, just time to scribble a few words, change, then out to lunch.

M-D is full of the excitement of the new, energised and almost attractive with her sparkly eyes and little-girl delight in it all. 'Everybody *talks* to you!' she said, amazed. 'There was this old man in a hat who had a metal-detector thing. He was picking up nickels and dimes as if they were fascinating archaeological finds! And he told me all about the War and all the people he killed and everything. They all say "Howyadoin'" and start talking to you as if they've known you *forever*! ...and there was this black girl whose car had broken down and she was waiting for the garage. And she told me all about her car and all about her husband and all about her garden and everything!...O Sally, I think I love it here!'

This worries me. After all, if she starts talking to all sorts of strangers she could come across a nutter. This country brims with them. And they've all got gun-racks and neuroses the like of which we never see in Britain.

There's also the thing about our being here incognito... if the news that a young English girl being here gets to the wrong ears...by now the police in every country will have her description; I assume they'll have realised that she was not one of the fifteen corpses found after the fire at the hospital, and neither was I. So by now they'll have realised that I must have run off with the child, and the Tweeds will leave no stone unsearched. And neither, I suppose, will Graham.

It will only take a few bright Americans to put two and two together, as cleverly as we tried to hide our tracks. I had to use my own passport to get into the country, putting Mary-Dyne down on it as Alice Alpert, my daughter.

We did try to be careful. We arrived in Houston on Continental. There I bought a ticket to Denver for both of us under false names. This was difficult! Especially when I insisted on paying cash, which no-one does in America. From there another flight to Omaha, this time separately under yet different names.

America is a big country. I hope this means it'll take them some time to trace us.

*

Lunch with Barbara in the Old Market area of the city. This is a sanitised cobbled jumble of crumbling Victoriana at the edge of the Missouri. Once it was a bustling smelly loud place, where merchants and cattlemen bickered and bartered and no doubt fought and shot each-other, the American national sport.

Omaha was converted from cattle to Insurance by dollar-eyed entrepreneurs, and the slaughter-houses and cattle trails shrank, and the wild men went to oblivion.

Then along came this massive food company who, in exchange for a grant of historic land to build their headquarters upon, cleaned everything up and built the Biggest Waterjet in America with a tiny loop of riverway upon which chugs a pastiche of a riverboat packed with thrilled, chattering tourists. So the warehouses were turned into expensive apartments or antique emporia or quiche restaurants or smart cafés.

The restaurant was crammed into a corner of one of these former warehouses, fake panelling fake beams and cast-iron columns. Or perhaps they are real...they certainly *look* fake.

We ate fish and chips ('To make you feel at home') and conversed politely for a time.

'I'm so glad to see how happy you and Chris are here,' I said, and she purred and giggled.

'That's true...' she said. 'Who would have believed *I'd* ever be so lucky...? Do you remember - '

Dreading a plunge into the pungent past I interrupted. 'I do, I do...' Our eyes met and we laughed, it felt as if for a moment our old friendship had flared up, like a forgotten old pimple.

'And the Research is going very well, from what I hear, isn't it?' I tried to sound ever-so casual. I had meant to catch her off-guard.

It didn't work.

I am going to have to accept! That Barbara and Chris must feel toward me like the recently rich person approached by dirt-poor relatives...spongers...

'Yes,' she said guardedly, a shadow over her face. 'Quite well. Of course it's far too early to tell...'

I took the warning. Leave it alone.

I switched my attention to Mary-Dyne, who had been happily and silently polishing-off a massive pile of potato twirly-things, cut so that they twirl into crazy double helixes. 'Enjoying yourself?' I asked, forcing the words out.

'It's great!' she said, 'I love this food!' The words spattered out between the squashed-up crisps.

'Good,' I said, and tried to smile despite the sink of depression.

Eventually I turned to Barbara again. 'How long?' I asked.

'How long what?' She asked,' How long before the compound is available to the public?'

'Yes. How long.'

She sighed. 'We don't really know. It'll depend on the tests. Luckily the FDA are giving permissions much quicker than they used to. But there are all sorts of factors...Five years? Ten years? I can't tell you.'

Then she looked at me with compassion, deep and sorrowful and I hated her for a brief minute, and I had to get up and mutter that I needed the toilet, and I went out into the sweltering heat of the non-air-conditioned street.

*

What the hell am I doing here. What's the point. Why did I listen to Tammy and her wild schemes. I'm going to die. There is no *deus ex machina.* I'm so damned TIRED all the time. I have fevers and headaches. I have nausea and pain. I can't eat.

Chris sees this of course. He suggested they admit me but I can't do that. I can't afford it for one thing. I can't pay by credit card because then they could track us down. I have some cash, about £4,000, raided from the account

Graham set up. I didn't take out insurance when we left and even if I had it wouldn't cover a disease I had before I left. I'm trapped here. I'm angry and frightened.

I'm too tired to sleep.

Oh God, I wished then, just for a little flash, that Graham was here...

Guilty guilty guilty

*

I fell asleep after I wrote that. I think, immediately after. Probably something to do with the Halcyon tablet Chris gave me.

It's 9 am. Outside on the balcony a very foreign bird - like a pigeon but with bright garish blue tailfeathers - is making ugly bright blue shrieking noises. This must be the last of the Passenger Pigeons, all of whose forebears were wiped out in the last century. If they all had penetrating shrieks like that it seems fair enough to me.

It's damned cold this morning. A chill breeze invades the room through the screen door. A tickle at the top of my nose threatens a cold. Horrible thought. I'm very tired, not ready to face anyone. I want to lie here. I want a cocoon. I want a sleeping pill that lasts until I die. Something light, with coloured dreams.

At least my internal clock is beginning to adapt to the time difference. Perhaps I should say to myself: this tiredness and lethargy is just jet-lag, and I'll start to feel much better soon.

Should I try to believe it?

I'll just lie here a while...then I can go and see what Mary-dyne is up to.

CHAPTER TWO

We had a barbeque this evening. The sky was burdened with dark clouds. The wind was chilly, edged with winter. I resented every moment I had to spend standing around with my hosts in the garden in the cold, a Cinzano (too sweet, I forgot that I hate the stuff) between my numbed fingers. I had made a very determined effort to look good for them. I wanted them to realise that I really value their kind attempts to make us feel at home.

So I primed myself with coffee before they got back from work, to make me buzzy and fun. Mary-dyne hung on my heels like a puppy, wanting to be noticed and loved and petted. She knows what I'm up to, though we haven't discussed it.

I was determined to put on a good show! The caffeine and my damned tiredness fought each-other and I won...(I don't know what the previous sentence means, but I like it.)

Chris slapped huge t-bone steaks onto the verdigris-streaked ancient gas griddle. The meat popped and sizzled. We stood around this friendly fire with our glasses in our hands, making forced witticisms. (Well, I did. All I wanted to do was sit down and there was nowhere to sit. I'll never understand why all the medics I know are so damned inconsiderate.)

Anyway, what did we talk about? Tammy and Graham, (I lied a lot of course, Chris and Barbara know nothing as yet about our adventures back home, perhaps they think we turned up in their lives by pure coincidence...I suppose they realise that we are here chasing a cure for me, like so many of the sad sick rich who'll chase any mere whisper of a cure anywhere in the world - then how do they explain M-D? They haven't asked anything about her, apart from the polite 'have you any brothers and sisters' and so on. They're very strange. I suppose they're so wrapped up in each-other that everyone they know is simply there to be the audience to their perfect wedded bliss...Cat!)

Eventually the dead cows' corpses had been burnt to Chris' satisfaction and we were finally allowed to take our places in the dining-room.

The long table is chrome and smoked glass. The crockery and cutlery looks strange here, Royal Doulton and Habitat, wedding souvenirs.

So this was it, I thought. I have been waiting for and training for this moment and so I stepped out of the wings. 'How's the research going then?' I addressed Chris directly, not wanting Barbara's foboffs.

Chris gave his wife an indulgent smile as if to say I Saw This Coming and Here it is. 'Oh not bad not bad. We're still waiting for FDA approval for the trial. We have no doubt they will.'

'I'll have to take you to the hospital, so that you can see for yourself,' Barbara offered.

'How does your treatment work?' I asked.

'It's not hard to explain.' Chris said. 'Imagine a switch, attached to the gene that causes the cancer.' he took a toothpick out of its glass container and held it between thumb and index finger. Then he began to drill it into a sugar-cube. 'We're trying to work out how to switch it off.' And he pushed it like a switch, making the cube break into powder.

'How do you do that?' I asked, looking guiltily at the mess.

Barbara took over. 'We're developing a new compound. It's fed to the patient intravenously, in a drip. So far it looks hopeful. It certainly works in the test-tube. All our monkeys are still alive, so toxicity doesn't seem to be a problem.'

'But you've tried it on a human,' I said, to remind her. 'I saw the article in the paper. He died.'

'Yes...but he didn't die as a result of our treatment. He was killed by the cancer.'

'Besides, ' Chris said, picking up the half-toothpick and using it to attack a stubborn piece of t-bone from between his front teeth. 'We only gave him a third of the dose.'

'But why?' I asked. I didn't mean it to sound despairing.

'We were only looking for side-effects, that sort of thing. The next trial will involve fifteen patients, double-blind - '

'I know,' I said, 'half get a placebo. Then you know if any improvement is related to the drug.'

'Oh no, we're just testing different levels, to make sure there are no problems.'

I thought for a moment. 'It's rather sad - ' I said.

'What?'

'Well, the patients you're using, they know they're trying something new. They'll be all full of hope, and most of them will die...'

Barbara gave a small sad smile. 'It's not very easy for us. Especially Chris, he's a real softy.' She squeezed his forearm. 'We get to like them, unfortunately...' she tripped over a thought and stopped herself.

'So there's a chance it works then?' I asked, shoving some salad into my mouth to cover myself.

'A chance...' Barbara said.

'More than a chance!' Chris interposed. 'Barbara will show you her graphs when you come to the hospital. We've got this new computer program. We put in the data from our work, compare it to the results of traditional chemo. It's quite amazing.'

'So what does it show?' I asked.

'Well, ' Chris said, 'summing it up, though our compound takes a little longer to work it works just as well...'

'I don't understand, ' I said, 'What's the point of your compound if it's only as good as chemotherapy?'

'Plenty!' Chris smiled benevolently. 'Firstly, there appear to be none of the side-effects. Secondly, and even more important, there's no return of the cancer!' He held a plucked cowbone up in the air. 'With chemo it often - nay, usually! - comes back...ours *kills* the little buggers. Or rather, turns 'em off. Cure!'

'See?' Mary-dyne - who I'd quite forgotten, tugged at my arm. She must have been listening with breath held, invisible girl. 'See?'

I wasn't in the mood for the left side of the t-bone. The other side had been a struggle to get down, each mouthful forced proof of how grateful I am for the food and accommodation etc etc etc. What etc.

'Marvellous,' I said brightly, with a smile I hope was suitably detached. I began to despair about quite how to bring my Request into the conversation.

I needn't have worried because Barbara is far more insightful than I give her credit for. She saw it coming. As soon as Tammy told her I was coming I suppose, and it was confirmed when I turned up on their doorstep.

Because she turned to me with that sickening compassionate look of hers again - the sort of look one uses when meeting a friend's new baby - 'Darling, we know what you're thinking, but you must listen to me now.'

What?' I said, wholly disconcerted.

'We know why you came here. It's obvious. We've talked about it for hours - ' Chris began, in an attempt to take over.

'I'll do this,' Barbara said as if to say, it's my job, I'm her friend, 'We're treating *Leukaemia*, dear. That's what our research is about. Your cancer...'

'I know,' I said, wanting to shut her up.

'It'll be years before...'

'I know, I know!'

'No, listen to me Sally. There's no way we're ready - '

'I've thought about all that!' I lost my self-possession then, for a moment. 'But couldn't you - ' Suddenly ashamed at my outburst I sat back and took a deep breath, feeling as if the next words I was about to say could have a critical effect on my life, 'I'm sorry, I'm sorry. I'm calm.' I took a sip of Cinzano. 'Just let me ask you a question. You said that ultimately this type of treatment could be extended to all cancers. Am I right?' Our hosts nodded. Barbara opened her mouth to speak, but I continued. 'Yes I know. The key word is *ultimately*. My question is this: how different would the compound have to be to treat *my* cancer?'

Barbara and Chris exchanged glances. 'It's rather complicated. In theory, the compound would be exactly the same. In fact, they're very interested in treatments for lymphoma here. But there is the issue of toxicity...if the gene is wrong, we'll have to redesign it...and get FDA permission to try it out...'

'We haven't tried it on any other cancers,' Barbara said flatly.

'So you can't say it wouldn't work! That's true isn't it?'

'Yes but - '

Silence. A big bubble of silence. They were thinking: she wants to be in the Trials. There won't be trials until after she's dead.

I was thinking: Offer me the drug! Steal it, borrow it, anything! I'm your old friend! You love me!

And if you don't I'll die!

And it'll be your fault...

Then I was ashamed and frightened that they had read my mind. 'I'm sorry,' I said, 'I never should have come. It's Tammy's fault. I shouldn't have listened to her...'

'We can't offer you a Trial.' Chris said it. 'It's too far off, we have applied for permission to test on Leukaemia. There's no way...'

I was crushed and shamed and humiliated. Somehow I managed an appearance of numbed dignity as I said I was tired and had to go to my bed now. Mary-dyne stood up with me and tagged along with me - unwelcome - upstairs. She kept saying 'They're so stupid. They're so cruel...' and eventually I snapped at her and asked her to leave me alone.

Now, lying in bed and writing this I'm trying to do something with the guilt. Not

*

Morning again. Mary-Dyne has just left my bed and gone to the bathroom. She came in as I was writing. She was very upset, more by my rejection of her than C&B's rejection of me...she begged me to sleep with her, and she lay next to me and hugged me like a frightened child. Begged me to be her mother. Told me she loved me. Pleaded with me not to die.

I have been very selfish. I have put Chris and Barbara in a terrible position. They're good people, no sense being cynical about that. They're really good people. I'm angry with them for being so good. And they're angry with me for having brought them face-to-face with what they're doing. Life and death and blood on their carpet. In their own den, their territory, their sacrosanct cave.

*

The park lay in the sun, humming with lazy insects. Students from the nearby University of Nebraska jogged around in skimpy shorts, mists of sweat invisible clouds trailing after them. Gays cruised each-other in cars. No-one lay on the grass, except us. Perhaps they know something we don't.

Strange foreign insects explored our secret places, hiding in moist warmth.

I had a brief feeling of self-consciousness when M-D and I arrived, stripped to skimpy swimsuits and lay on our towels. Is this sort of thing *done* out here, in the puritanical Midwest? Showing our puffy English bodies to strangers?

What the hell, we're strangers here and I need sun.

'So what do we do now?' Mary-Dyne asked, when we'd reached that point in the sunbathing routine when it has just become boring. (With me that's usually about ten minutes after I lie down. Especially if I haven't remembered a book.)

'I don't know,' I answered. 'We can't stay here much longer, that's for sure.'

'We could travel! she said brightly, 'Explore America. Look for the heart of the USA!'

'Mmm.' I said.

She sighed, and then a thought gripped her. 'You mean no. You mean you're not - well enough...' Sorrow and fear of loss was gripping her again.

'Perhaps it's time to go back to the UK and face the music. If we explain to the police why we ran off, maybe we can scare your wicked uncle and aunt into behaving themselves...you can live happily ever after and I - '

'You! You'll die! You'll leave me!'

'I - ' I sighed, not without a hitch in the throat 'I will die happily and quietly in the arms of my loving husband, safe in the green and pink and beige...'

Mary-Dyne went into a deep sulk, sat up in a crouch, arms clasped around legs, head buried in knees, so that I almost missed what she said and I had to ask her to repeat herself, because I just felt as if the sun was about to crash into my head.

'I *said*, they're not my uncle and aunt...'

'What do you mean? Explain what you said!'

She lifted her head, stared at a softball game as if she was looking at it...and she said again, 'They're not my uncle and aunt. They're my parents.' She stiffened, as if expecting a blow.

My brain did a double somersault. Then some squat-thrusts. Then a manic pirouette. Then it fell down and my mouth screamed '*WHAT*?'

Why am I smiling as I write this? Why do I have this terrible mad desire to laugh?

I didn't feel this way in the park! Do I need to describe how I felt?

Jean Tweed had told me the truth when she said that her daughter is a pathological liar, a dweller in fantasy worlds. Someone who adjusts reality to fit in with their dreams.

I want to try hard to remember what she said next, because after I've written it down I want to think about it: Plenty:

Something like this, (I wasn't listening to her by then, I was listening to my internal monologue going Oh No, Not This and This means that... and that...) , 'Please forgive me, you must forgive me, I'm so sorry ..'(quite a lot of that) '...I hate them so much, don't you understand? They've always treated me like a *problem*, not a *person*. They don't like me at all! I had to get away, they wanted to put me in a special school, I would have died! I couldn't! I couldn't!' She risked a glance at me then and when she saw my expression, 'You are the first real friend I ever had! Don't *look* at me that way!'

'You lied to me.' I said cruelly. I felt very cruel. She had entered my life and torn it up with her lies. She'd disrupted and destroyed the lives of all those other people...when I think! - of it now! - It makes me angry again, how *could* she...

I could have killed her.

Had she not then run away, fleet-footed as a twelve-year old should be, leaving the sodden heavy cloud of her misery behind her...

...with me...

*

It's 4pm and still no sign of her. I'm lying on my bed feeling blanked and exhausted (remembering that Doc whatsname said that after all the radiation treatment I've had I should avoid the sun. I can't remember why.) Writing is hard. I have a headache. Something to do with the sun, probably. And the tension. How do I feel about Mary-Dyne - ? I must start calling her Annie. Mary-Dyne was a cheap badly-drawn character in a Mills & Boon.

Apart from still wanting to kill her - preferably *before* we met - I feel very sorry for her indeed. I was an only child too. I also had remote, apparently uncaring parents. I also had a very busy fantasy life in which, in my loneliness, I was a princess, I was a model, I was the owner of an airline...the difference is, I always knew that my dreams were only dreams. Did I lie to strangers about myself?....Oh I know I did, thinking about it. Usually to other little girls whose admiration I craved.

What if she doesn't come back? Where the hell *is* the girl? ...this is America, crazies everywhere... she could be lying dead in the creek, her raggedy hair streaming out behind her like Ophelia's...the picture frightens me, but doesn't seem to dilute my anger very much.

Serve her right! (Scratch that out)

*

We've just searched the park. Chris, Barbara and I. The sun was setting when gave up. Now C & B want to get the police onto it and I have begged them to give her another hour. I'm regretting that. If she's been hurt I'll never forgive myself. But I can't have the police involved. The whole story will come out. She - Annie - is such an independent little soul, she's good at looking after herself. She's probably hiding behind a bush, it's getting cold, she'll shiver a bit, then she'll find her way home.

Please.

*

I must have dozed off after writing the last section, because suddenly there she was sitting on the bed, tapping me gently on my shoulder. Her face was lit up with excitement, all lit up with the Plan...

If I write it down now, that could be dangerous. Evidence. If it goes wrong...

I wasn't interested at first. The whole thing sounds impossible! Ridiculous! If I write it down I'll realise how impossible...

I have to think about this!

I want to say, though, that I do think she's absolutely crazy...I have to think, wake myself, think. While I think, I'll write this:

I was so relieved to see her face, yet angry at her expression of delight and air of conspiracy. Frustrated at her inability to understand how worried I had been. All she would talk about was her Idea. The scheme she'd dreamed up as she crouched in a dank secret subway under the main road.

Eventually I had no choice but to listen to her.

I listened to her.

C & B hadn't called the police, so that was alright.

I listened to her.

I'm going to go on calling her Mary-Dyne now, because that's who she has become for me. She is my true friend and she loves me. I'm not used to being loved like this, so unselfishly. It's like the fully accepting love of a dog - I don't mean that to sound patronising. I've always found it hard to divorce the experience of love from its expression in sex, mainly I suppose because I had such an arid childhood. My friendships were few, and that's all they were - friendships. I always found it hard to understand how close some of the girls at school were to one-another. I never really had a best friend', the way some of them did. Then in college I had my two companions, Barbara and Tammy - we were close, but we didn't love each-other.

This bond between this child and me feels so strong and real, I'm probably the first person she has been wholly honest and open with. Laugh! She opened herself to me when she confessed her Big Lie. She really showed that she trusts me. She dropped her fantasy, let me see her Real Self and that feels like a great privilege. Some of our conversation was about that: lying to friends, truth, fantasy ('But you know the truth now, and that shows...I'll *never* lie to you again, I give you my very bestest *Word*...')

Ramble ramble ramble. Switch off, mind. Relax toes relax calves re

CHAPTER THREE

Good morning and a happy Saturday to you. We're all going to an Antiques Warehouse place ('Only if you feel well enough' - yes I do but I do hate people saying that, I don't want to stop them having a good time...I don't feel too bad this morning, I slept well and despite a rather sharp headache and shrunken appetite I'll manage the day...Yet I can't help feeling that every day is just a little bit worse. I can feel a slow, sad slippage. I'll act, behave, be well!)

The others are washing themselves or standing in line for the bathroom or getting dressed.

Breakfast was happy and laughing and calm, especially after M-D and I announced our intention of returning to the UK within a week. I made a little prepared speech, like this: 'Chris, Barbara, we have an announcement.'

'Go on, announce, 'Chris said, his forced smile looming at me over the huge pancake he was slipping off the frying-pan onto my plate.

'You've been absolutely marvellous to us,' I said, adjusting the thing on my plate so that it was more symmetrically arranged. 'You couldn't have been more welcoming, and I do understand what sort of effect my turning up here had on you.'

'Don't be silly darling,' Barbara said, 'it's lovely to have old friends turning up. It happens so seldom - '

'You know what I mean. I tried emotional blackmail on you, and I regret that briefly. I hope you will accept this as an apology over what happened the other night. I truly do understand that you would do anything you could to help me, and I'm sorry that there is nothing you *can* do. There are still things I haven't tried yet, new treatments. As you said a little while ago, Chris, I haven't yet given chemotherapy a proper go. So we're going back.'

C & B exchanged one of their glances. Which said, what a relief. 'So soon?' Barbara said lamely.

'Oh, I think it would be a good idea if I start treatment as soon as possible. There's still a chance I can survive this. We'll be leaving just as soon as we can get a flight.'

'Well, don't make it *too* soon,' Barbara said (as predicted)

'Well...' I said, as if wanting to be convinced, 'a *few* more days wouldn't hurt...'

'Oh please can we stay just a bit longer,' M-D begged. 'I do love it here. And I'd just adore to see Dodge City and Lincoln and Kansas City...I've never been to America before!' Well said little one.

'Stay a week,' Chris said. 'As your medical advisor I'm sure another week won't adversely affect your condition.'

'All right,' I said, yielding graciously to their friendly pressure. 'We'll leave next Saturday.'

'Oh goody!' M-D clapped her hands. 'Oh goody!'

*

So we went to the Antiques Warehouse. An hour's drive up a highway packed with mechanical Americana, mostly BIG. M-D was delighted by the trucks - vast, terrifying, murderously efficient, all done up in burgundy and gold and coachlines, square menacing and somehow gloriously old-fashioned, like massively blown-out-of-proportion Model-T Fords.

The rule around here is that everyone drives exactly 10mph over the speed limit. This is apparently what one can get away with, in an unspoken agreement twixt cops and others. As a result, everyone drives at exactly this speed, so that if you're in a bunch of traffic there's no overtaking and if any one vehicle should have a problem there'd be one almighty scrunch.

...Everything is BIG. The Antiques Warehouse spreads itself over acres. It's all filled with a variety of sad old crap, forties, fifties, sixties. Antiques here have an air of sadness and hardship. Everything well used, ill cared for. So unlike the stuff back home, which feels solid and smug and happy and loved.

I bought a pair of forties sunglasses (9 dollars). C & B bought a Mission oak sideboard. It'll look stupid in their chrome and glass dining room. How lovely I said.

How lovely said M-D.

(Tired. Tired. Tired!)

*

The atmosphere in the house has become all fluffy and pink and cuddly. We're all such Good Friends. Good enough for me to ask at dinner for M-D and I to visit the Hospital on Monday.

Barbara let a fleeting expression of uncertainty cross her face as she said, 'Are you sure? Won't that be - ' (She'd wanted the whole subject of my cancer to go away)

'Oh you mustn't worry about my getting emotional or anything like that,' I blandly reassured her. 'I just want to show Mary-Dyne what you're doing. She's so interested.'

'So interested' Mary-Dyne said.

*

Today, Sunday, I dragged myself long to the Old Market again, then to the Art Gallery where I pretended to enjoy a display of Western Art, a celebration of the macho myths of Middle America, tough, stupid men revelling in killing and screwing and drinking when they weren't chasing cows and bulls about. This is America's bloody heritage, these arrogant despoilers and murderers and thieves.

'How exciting,' I said.

'How thrilling and *manly*!' M-D enthused.

How tiring

*

C & D beamed. What good hosts they are.

*

I'm feeling better already.

*

As promised, I've been thinking.

*

Monday: M-D and I spent the whole day at the Hospital. We saw the lab, where Barbara showed the awestruck child her slides of the Lifeeaters. M-D was as angry at them as I was when I first saw them. Little buggers, we said in unison.

We met some of the patients too. M-D 'played' - if that's the word - with a small, masked, bald girl called Kirsty. The mask was to protect her bone-marrow which had recently been returned to her from becoming infected by our germs.

It seems they have to take out the bone-marrow before giving the full chemo treatment, because it destroys everything. Everything. Including, they hope, the cancer. Then they give the bone-marrow back and she starts to get better.

(Barbara explains it this way: 'First we kill the patient with lethal radiation and chemotherapy, then we resurrect them.')

Sitting with Kirsty, watching her and M-D gaily reciting nursery rhymes has reinforced my resolve, dissolved my anxieties.

Poor Kirsty. I hope she survives.

*

Now to detail: draw the layout of the Oncology suite....

The nurses' station is manned *all* of the time.

The labs occupy the Ground Floor. Draw the relevant section

*

A good day's work. Which has, as I said, convinced me that I cannot and will not allow the doctors to savage my body with their chemicals and lethal rays. The section labelled A in Diagram 1 is where patients wait for their chemo. I saw horrors there, freakshow horrors which twisted my heart... I have to describe: People of all ages sit in this room in special chairs designed for them: each with its bowl in the arm, for sudden vomits. Each with a pan for urgent evacuations. Their white hands clasp copies of USA Today, shaking too much to read. Heads with varying amounts of hair, the bald patches white running with blue veins full of chemicals. Faces calm or ravaged, while brave, furtive attempts at conversation hang in the grey air.

There is some laughter. Cancer patients have their own special type of humour. The jokes vary from the trivial to the nauseous. The common theme is hospital and doctor inefficiency, bizarre side-effects of the treatments, even death itself...I wish I could remember jokes! Because Chris told me some of them, and they're sickeningly funny...

Patients also invade the Restaurant or Canteen or whatever they call it, like white premonitions in their hospital gowns they sit and chat and pick at salads. I saw two old men playing chess so slowly it seemed as if it might be interesting to bet on which would come first, death or checkmate.

Kirsty accompanied us to the canteen. She was insistent about this and we found out why: she is addicted to just the sort of ice-cream that makes her puke. Which had been forbidden to her. Which she didn't tell us.

CHAPTER FOUR

All the leaves left the trees overnight. Apparently there was a huge windstorm. I must have been sleeping fantastically soundly, because I heard nothing. Autumn has sneaked up on us suddenly, and though I did notice that some of the leaves had spots of brown, I hadn't considered the possibility of summer ending.

Now the ground is carpeted with leaves. Most are quite green. The trees obviously agreed with me.

I feel as if I'm being rushed, not ready for the future...they tell me winters here are nightmares, portents of the next ice age. Last winter the temperature in parts of the state fell to minus 23. Here in Omaha, Chris told us at breakfast, it was minus fourteen for two months.

'So tell me,' Barbara asked conveniently, 'what are you guys planning on doing today?'

I played with my egg, allowing my eyes to meet M-D's for an instant. 'How would you feel about letting us use your car?' I asked. Sensing the hesitation of resistance I added quickly, 'Mary-Dyne and I are considering exploring the environs. Maybe going to Dodge City. That kind of thing.'

'Well... ' Barbara said, 'I suppose - Chris?' I wish she wouldn't *defer* to him all the time.

'If you're sure you'll be happy driving on the wrong side of the road...' Chris said, with an uncertain smile. His blue Chev is one of the prides of his life.

'We'll give you a ride to work, of course,' I offered.

'That will be necessary,' Chris smiled, 'You do the driving. It'll give you some supervised practice.'

195

So M-D and I drove them to work. Chris sat tense and pale next to me muttering all the way, advice and commands. (I was puzzled when he made me go through a red light, turning right. Apparently this is legal, which seems quite sensible to me.)

'You'll be alright won't you? Got the map and everything?' he asked as we dropped them off.

'No problem,' I said.

Then we drove around the corner, stopped and spread the map out to plot the immediate area. Then we spent a happy, absorbed morning driving around all the streets near the hospital, marking out routes.

Lunch in the Old Market - a Continental place, where I picked at Bavarian smoked ham on rye. M-D ate an elaborate salad with feta and some razor-thin slices of exotic meat, followed by roll mops. These Americans mix *every* kind of food together!

After lunch we drove to the airport. I am getting the hang of driving on the right. We bought tickets with our waning cash. Returned to Omaha just in time to fetch our host and hostess from the hospital.

'So how was Dodge City?' Barbara asked brightly, as Chris politely nudged me out of the driver's seat.

'Great!' M-D exclaimed enthusiastically. 'Isn't it amazing! The whole wild west in one place!'

I laughed merrily. M-D's Major Flaw (her Lying Tendency) is becoming rather useful.

*

I was woken early this morning by the sounds of loud male banter. Went downstairs in my nightgown to find out who why and what.

'Morning Sally,' Chris said, 'sorry we woke you. This is Sam, he's come to do some work on the house.'

'Hi Sam' I said.

'Howyadoin' Sam greeted me in Midwestern, a massive grin splashing across his broad face.

Sam is a big, wide, bluff, loud local. He was wearing long shorts, a plaid shirt, and he carried a box of tools. He's a really big man, whose fat is largely muscle - or is it the other way round? Massive hands, pink, childish face which would be cute if it weren't for the droopy, quite unathome moustache.

'Fine,' I said.

Sam gave me a couple more seconds of his grin and then turned it on Chris. 'Wal,' he said, 'Better go get the stuff.'

'What stuff?' Chris asked.

'Heck, you want that washstand done don't you? Gotta go order it.'

'There's a telephone over there,' Chris said, brow darkening.

'Wait on, you don't want just *any* ole washstand do ya? It's gotta be good, right? 'Sides, Tuesday ain't my best day.' He turned the grin up a notch or two with the professional charmer's typical conviction that their cutey smile would get them anything. This, with a brilliant dollop of absolute frankness, normally does the trick.

Chris was disarmed, and my respect for him shrank. 'Uh - I see,' he said.

'Back later. No point getting back before the afternoon, I guess.'

'Why not?' Chris asked, recovering a little.

'Wal, time I've got into town and parked and checked out what they got and ordered the best there is for you it'll be about lunchtime, right? So lunchtimes I drop in to my brother Nick, he's working not far from here. We'll have a couple beers, that sort of thing. Then I'll hurry back. OK? You have a good day now,' he said, making a fast exit.

Chris turned to me, shaking his head with exasperation.

'Obviously a paid-up member,' I said.

'Of what?'

'International Union of Plumbers Builders and Allied Trades,' I said, 'operating according to the Official Code.'

'I know what you mean,' Chris laughed. 'Minimum work, maximum money...would you mind being in after lunch to let him in?'

Damn! Plans disrupted. 'I - I suppose I could,' I said.

*

So M-D and I spent the morning on an elongated planning session. I sometimes suspect there may be a God. It's strange how well things seem to *fit*, sometimes.

'Kirsty is a gift,' M-D said.

'So it seems!'

'I'll have to spend some time with her, work on her.'

'Go along to the Hospital this afternoon. I'll give Barbara a ring. Explain to her that you've become attached to the child. You can take a cab.'

'Fine,' she said. 'And what will you be doing?'

'I've a strange feeling,' I said sagely, 'we've been given another gift.'

'Oh?'

*

I sat at the desk, writing away. Sam measured windows. 'You're British?' he asked as he carelessly prised a storm-window away from its seat.

'That's right,' I answered.

'Vacation?'

I turned from my writing, smiled brightly at him. 'Sort of,' I said. 'Part business.'

'It'd have to be I guess. Very few people come here for a vacation.' he laughed, in gentle deprecation of his home town. 'Don't know why. I love this place.'

'Lived here all your life?' I asked.

'Man and boy. It's a great place to grow up. I've seen the world, now, don't mistake me.'

'Oh?'

'Five years in the marines. We went all over the place. Far East, Yurp, I seen it all. Funny thing though. No place like home, that's what they all say.'

'That's what they say,' I agreed.

He went to another cracked window and whipped out his measuring tape. 'Every one of these is different,' he said in explanation. 'It's these old houses. Nothin' standard.'

I laughed. 'It's strange for me to hear a twenties house described as *old*,' I said.

'Oh sure you got much older houses in Yurp.' (He *does* say Yurp.) 'I seen 'em. *Real* old.'

'That's true,'

'So what's the Business you doin'?'

'I'm a writer,' I said. 'A novelist.'

'Gee!' he said, genuinely impressed. 'My mother was a writer too. Detective stories, science fiction, that kind of stuff. She wrote under the name Harry Hawks. See, she wouldn't have been accepted if they knowed she was a woman. So she like invented the name. Ever hear of her?'

'Sure! - ' I said, with feigned enthusiasm, 'Didn't she write that - what was it called - ?'

'Martian Invaders? You thinkin of that one, I'll bet. It was her best known. So what are you writing?'

I thought fast. 'Kind of adventure-romance. It's all about these international crooks who do this - uh - heist in a midwest town. I chose Omaha because my friends live here.'

'Wow, ' he said, 'that's great. I know plenty about this city. You should ask me. For background and stuff.'

'I will,' I said. 'Fancy a coffee?'

*

Well, I asked for it. Sam is, annoyingly, as garrulous as I expected him to be. By the end of the afternoon I had found out everything I didn't want to know about his ex-wife, his years in the marines, the petty crimes he'd tangled himself up in, the contents of his gun-rack.

The one thing that impresses me is his ability to work and talk at the same time. I feel a small twinge of guilt for having described him as a member of the International Union. When he works, he sure works.

Sam was married to his first wife for four years, after he left the marines. Then he met this wild woman who was involved in a motorcycle gang. This must have been the early sixties, before the Hell's Angels and the Wild bunch. he rescued her, stole her from the Big Man, the gang leader. Ran away with her. Was pursued. (Haven't I seen a movie with just this plot? He *can't* be another M-D.) Beat the guy in a fair fight. Loved her, lived with her, 'till she ran away...Sam can't understand why she did this.

My host and hostess have gone out to dinner, taking M-D with them. I pleaded tiredness and I am feeling tired. All the usual feelings, I am getting used to them as the monster devours more and more of me. My glands seem to have shrunk to about half ping-pong ball size. They make me feel ridiculous, clown-like. I wish I could joke about it, like those others at the Hospital.

I've nibbled at the TV dinner Barbara left me. Unfortunately I made the mistake of reading the list of ingredients as the thing lay steaming on the plate like a predatory slime-monster. I binned it all, it'll lie in the bin glooping and slurping until it finally finds a place of plenty in the dump.

*

I don't want to write about how I feel all the time. I just need to eat properly! I'm tired all the time, though the pills are helping with energy, it's like something is sneaking up on me...I remember years ago, at Uni, a boy took me to bed and promised me a day in a music studio – the old promise, 'you've got a great voice! I can make you famous! And after he'd extracted his payment (he wasn't bad, just needy) I helped him make a single. A real one. It sold a hundred copies in Germany or somewhere. It was called 'the Beast of Sudden Trouble Stalks us All'. Yes it does...

*

The bell rang ding dong as I was writing the above. And Tammy and George poured in through the door, back into my life.

Is this a nuisance or a blessing???

Tammy is looking sleek and kittenish, well-fucked. George is getting just a tad fat. This is aesthetically unforgiveable, but it gives me a glimpse into his likely future: In ten years time, pretty boy, you'll be sleek and smug and balding. This cheers me up. Bastard! How dare you choose Tammy over me!

They came all the way here to warn us. The police are, as Tammy said melodramatically, 'Onto' us. She had a visit from them. It seems the Tweeds have decided that I 'kidnapped' the girl. The police are not convinced: they link my disappearance with the 'Spireslea Scam', as the tabloids are calling it, suggesting that I was in league with Joan and Harry and have run off to Brazil with the ill-gottens. Well, really! As if twentysomething thousand pounds would be enough to make me run off with those scumbags... (all this American TV is having an unfortunate effect on my prose)

It occurs to me that they said nothing about the fire. I must ask.

Tammy saw Graham before they left. He's back home, brooding and agonising. She says he's desperately worried about me. I can't deny that this causes me to feel a prick of guilt and sorrow. Whatever Graham is - staid, boring, over meticulous, flabby of stomach and head - he is certainly sincere, feels things deeply, loves me.

All right, while I do feel guilty for having left, I still can't feel love. In fact, his making me feel guilty breeds resentment. How dare he. I CANNOT BE CONFINED IN A CAGE, dear Graham.

I wish I could send him some sort of message to reassure him.

'So why do you say they're onto us?' I asked Tammy, as I gave them coffee and biscuits. (Which they wolfed down. Apparently the airline gave them a meal at lunchtime and nothing more until 8.30 in the evening! Probably in the hope that the time-change would have confused all the passengers so much, they wouldn't know when to feel hungry.)

That Tweed has hired a private Dick,' Tammy said. 'It's almost as if they genuinely love the child...'

'Tammy,' I said, 'It's quite likely they do.'

'What do you mean?'

(I get the horrible feeling that I'm translating the conversation into American. This is probably symptomatic of my adopting any accent that's around me. Must stop it.)

So I told them that M-D's story was entirely bogus...

I don't know if this was the right thing to do.

'WHAT?' George was stunned. 'You mean it was all a lie? They weren't out to kill her?'

'No,' I said, ashamed on behalf of the child. 'You must try to understand.' I said, 'Her lying wasn't malicious, or mischievous - it was more than that - '

'So what was it? She deserves a good thrashing!' George said vehemently.

'I know what Sally is getting at,' Tammy said, inching closer to him on the sofa. (If she got any closer she'd come out the other side). 'The child was very unhappy. Felt unloved. Was just trying to get some attention.'

'I see those psychology lectures at college weren't wasted on you,' I smiled.

'Is there anything else to eat?' George changed the subject.

*

We talked solidly for two hours, despite the visitors' fatigue, and mine.

I told them everything. As I could have predicted, George was horrified and Tammy was delighted. George is a closet conservative. Not so closet. And to think I thought him homosexual! - not to say, of course, that there aren't conservative (and Conservative) homosexuals. One of my gay friends at Bristol was a Tory and a high Anglican. Paul Beamish. My Worthy Opponent.

George's conventionality raises my hackles. And I like that. A further excuse for feeling relieved that my fantasies concerning him never turned into a tacky relationship. Happily-ever-after with George could well be worse than caged-in-a-Portnoy with Graham. At least Graham doesn't argue about everything.

'I think it's perfectly shocking. Apart from being extremely illegal, I find it quite immoral as well.'

'I don't believe this!' Tammy expostulated. 'I know you're slightly prudish - but just think about everything we've done so far! Like helping Sally to escape the country with a teenage runaway - involving yourself in that whole silly spying thing - '

'None of that was *immoral*,' George said sternly. 'After all we believed that what we were doing was for the sake of a child. A poor, threatened child as we thought. Who turns out to have been nothing but a filthy little liar all the time!'

'For heaven's sake!' Tammy said, drawing away from him.

'Which makes all this cloak-and-dagger very silly and futile.'

Tammy sat herself up on the arm of the sofa, a habit she has when she feels threatened. 'And was it futile for Sally to have come here, when this is the best place for her to find a cure to save her life?'

'Oh I can understand that,' George said patronisingly, 'but what I cannot understand is this Plan of hers.' They were now discussing me as if I wasn't there. 'Surely you can't consider helping her with this? It's the most dreadful idea. Can you imagine what will happen to us if it goes wrong?'

'Don't worry about that,' I interjected. 'M-D and I have covered every possible - '

'You say it's immoral. How can you believe that it's not immoral to withhold a possibly life-saving medicine from a *friend*?' Tammy was pink with indignation and, possibly, disillusionment.

'That's not the issue - '

'And would it be immoral for me to help my friend to get that cure?' she challenged.

'At *any* cost??' George riposted. 'Besides, that's what you said the last time, with this ridiculous lying child. And look where it gets us.'

I was terrified, mind in a spin. If George thinks this way, he could blow the whole thing.

I staged a weeping fit. It seemed the only thing to do, and Tammy came over to me, hugged me and promised me that everything would be all right.

Then we heard our hosts' car come gliding up the drive. And as their happy, chatty, satisfied voices leaked out of the opening car doors, Tammy begged George, 'Don't say anything about this. Please, please George. If you love me.'

George, feeling guilty for having upset me, reluctantly agreed.

*

Greetings and introductions. Chris and Barbara took the new arrivals on the chin, brave souls. Their smiles and invitations were rather forced, but well-meant.

M-D consented happily to give up her room to the new arrivals and to sleep in the lounge. Not realising that one of them is probably a serpent in the nest.

And I am lying awake, despite two valium, thinking, writing. I can hear whispered arguing next-door, though I can't make out the words. The jury is out. Fifty-fifty split. Here I am, waiting for the verdict.

Death sentence?

*

I slept until midday. I probably dropped off eventually at around five am. And I slept beautifully, though dream-ridden. I wish I could remember my dreams... my first thought on waking was 'Whotta journey!" What journey?

I didn't enjoy waking up, especially when the memory of last night came back like Mad Max, barbed, saw-toothed, dangerous.

I could get to hate George.

There are voices downstairs, male and female. I think I'll go down and get something to eat, find out what's happening.

Getting up and dressed is going to be difficult.

*

The voices belonged to Tammy and Sam. When I came into the kitchen, there they were over coffee like conspirators.

'Morning Sally,' Tammy said brightly. 'Sleep well?'

'Howyadoin' Sam said.

'Fine, ' I said blearily. Then, 'Where's George? Where's Mary-Dyne?'

'He's gone for a walk,' Tammy answered, and then to answer the concern on my face, 'Oh don't worry. He's put a twenty-four-hour moratorium on it. He's deciding what to do.'

'Good,' I said.

'Want some toast? Sam has been telling me about his fascinating life.'

'Yes please', I said, seating myself at the horrible formica table. 'And some of that coffee. Please.'

'Yes, it's *really* fascinating,' Tammy said meaningfully.

She wanted me to express an interest. 'I know,' I said, 'He's told me.'

'Heck, it's all in the past now,' Sam said modestly. 'I was telling this lady here so she can use some of it in her writing.'

'Writing?' I asked, then, remembering the previous day's lie, 'Oh yes, for my novel.' I fired a warning glance at Tammy.

'I've changed a whole lot since then. I'm respectable now, know what I mean. Got a nice house, little business. Go to church every Sunday. No-one who knew me ten years ago would ever believe that!' He guffawed, his innocent little-boy face creasing up, showing his age.

'So,' I said wearily, humouring him, 'You've got a dark and mysterious past. So what are the parts you didn't tell me about yesterday?'

Tammy bustled around, humming to herself as she made coffee and toast. Sam filled in.

I confess I hardly listened. I don't know why Tammy wanted me to be so interested, some reasons of her own. Sam rambled on about how he was involved in smuggling drugs over the Mexican border, shot a man once, played hell in Atlantic City, more of that sort of boastful macho bullshit. Tammy winked happily at me once or twice from behind him. Interrupted once to ask where C&B keep their sugar.

All very wearying. I spend so much of my life humouring people.

'So you see,' Tammy interrupted him eventually (two cups of coffee and four slices of toast eventually), 'Sam's just the sort of person we need, don't you agree?'

'What?' I asked, having lost track of what was going on. I had been thinking about something else, my automatic tactic when confronted by the boring.

'I said, Sam could be useful, don't you agree?'

I had a flash of fear then, realising what she was doing. I don't want any more people involved! The more people, the more danger.

As is *proven* by the involvement of George.

'Look, Tammy, I think we should talk about this alone, don't you?'

She followed me into the garden. A chilly wind went straight through my dressing-gown. I hugged myself for warmth. 'Tammy, are you thinking about involving this Sam person in the Plan? It's a crazy idea, crazy!' - then I stopped myself, because that was exactly what I had thought of doing...

But that was before Tammy and George arrived! That changed everything...besides, I have to discuss it with M-D. She's part of this.

But then she said, 'Um Sally, it's too late for that. I've told him everything already. We've been talking for hours. I really trust him.'

'Oh no.'

'Listen, you mustn't worry. When I told him your story, he was so angry! All his life he's wanted to be the Knight in White Armour, only he's never had the chance before. You should hear the story about his ex-wife - '

'I already have,' I said.

'Well then, you know what sort of person he is. I promise you he's totally committed. Especially now he's seen you - ' She stopped her flow, embarrassed.

'I see,' I said sadly. I knew what she meant. I must look a terrible haunted red-eyed sight in my dressing-gown and unmade-up face, at midday...God I've let myself go. Let myself down! I need a red dress and high heels and blood-red lipstick. One day I will look good again. One day I will.

'We'll use him. I have many ideas, many. Contingency plans. I think you and - what must I call her now? Mary-Dyne or Annie? - any way, the girl, are doing the right thing. The only thing. And I'm going to help you all the way darling. I am.' She held me by the shoulders, staring into my eyes. Hers were brimming with tears, which made me very uncomfortable, because I know how seldom Tammy is moved by anything. I have to believe that she really means it. She held me close, kissed me on the cheek and I wept too.

BOOK IV

CHAPTER ONE

On a plane again. So much has happened since I stopped writing! I had to stop, you see. The danger of this Journal being used as evidence against us was too great. Besides, everything happened so fast. And now, sitting in this aircraft in Houston, waiting to take off, heart-in-mouth - I'm not afraid of a crash or anything like that - it's just that until we are out of the US, we're still in danger.

But when we take to the skies, ah, when we roar and tumble through the air, I'll be free! And clutching my flight bag, I'll be the freest thing in these wide skies...

I'm sitting next to a window, on my right. Through which I can see the solid bulk of a Virgin Airlines jumbo. It looks so sleek and clean, yet raffish with that WW2 image of a flying Esther Williams (forties supergirl), a wry comment on virginity - and mid-century male fantasies... I'd much rather be on that 'plane, staring through my window at the vast tubular rusting Continental Airlines workhorse in its red and white livery, as it fills with moms n pops and backpackers and children.

I'm looking forward to takeoff. That stomach-grabbing wrench as 'plane ploughs through protesting sky.

(There's a babble of Arabic around me. Why?)

My companion snores. That's fine by me.

The air hostesses look like Sunset Strip hookers with Fawcett-Major hair, festooned with costume jewellery. Or sultry Southern belles. Clichés in high heels.

Hurry up, time!

Announcements: 'Good afternoon ladez an Genmen, my name is Scott Mackenzie and I'm your Flight Manager on this trip...' What happened to the Captain? Is there one? Are we flying-by-wire? Or has the Captain been demoted to the status of the driver of this 'bus. Flying isn't an adventure any more. It's just business.

My heart is fluttering. Take deep breaths. Another valium? No, I'll try natural methods for a bit more. Then the valium.

Read something. In my personal seat-pocket, a mail-order catalogue. 'Continental Sky Mail'. So that even at extythousand feet I can go shopping! Who could be without, for example, the 'Best Nose-Hair Remover' or 'Tools for Pleasurable Walks' (walking sticks) or The young Ted Williams Autographed Print'. Hello Ted, whoever you are. I'll bet your writing hand aches, with all the signing you have to do.

...we're moving backwards at last. The wing looks rusty, grimy. Yet I feel completely secure. This craft is *solid*, reliable, faithful, indestructible.

The tarmac is wet. We're stopped again. They're playing the safety video, which everyone cheerfully ignores. There's no going back now, no going back!
...moving forward now...I love this... stop... move... feels like being on a large ocean liner in a light swell... slow... stop again... I crave coffee... the belles are handing out headsets, fussing up and down the plane, breasts bobbing, jewellery flashing...moving again..turning now, building power...come *on*! ... pointing our nose up a runway dotted

with red and yellow jewels of winking light... now ... NOW ...*MORE!*

WHEW

Goodbye America.

*

I can tell the whole story now, here in the clouds where no-one can get to me. I must tell it properly, in sequence...first I'll pop a pill, as coffee has finally arrived. What a pill. What a *delicious* pill.

Let me just check back on how much you know so far. Ah yes, Tammy was hugging me on the chilly lawn. George was out walking, having deep discussions with himself, trying to decide on whether to kill me or not.

M-D was at the Hospital, plotting things with her tiny acolyte.

Chris and Barbara were in the lab, congratulating themselves on some promising data.

You will have guessed by now that our Plan was to steal the Compound. And you would be right.

*

There were several obstacles to our carrying out the Plan. The chief of which was security.

As you can imagine, the place was sealed as tight as a bank vault. There were drug companies all over the world who would kill to get the formula for the Compound as, despite the best efforts of the University of Omaha, rumours of Chris and Barbara's successes were running riot throughout the Cancer world.

So our main problems were three:

1. Security: All research notes, formulae and the Compound itself were locked in a safe overnight. The lab was sealed and alarmed, the only entry being by a coded lock system. Then the Research Building itself was locked up, guarded by mean-looking men with guns.

2. Escape: Even if we were successful in stealing the Compound, we would still have to get out of the country.

3. George: My life was in his hands! (Or rather, mouth)

This latter worried me terribly that day. You can imagine what was going through my mind when Tammy told me that he had gone for a walk! I was convinced he was going to the police. He would wreck everything, he'd have them swarming all over us, we'd be deported and then...

I pulled myself away from Tammy's arms and told her about this fear. That sentence reads so rational! Though I probably sounded nearly hysterical, and felt it too. 'George will ruin everything Tammy. He's so *priggish*, so damned *moral*, so - '

'Pedantic, dogmatic, arrogant? That just shows how much you know about him. Listen: ' she took my hands in hers and gave me her Charming mischievous Look, the one she uses on men to get them to do whatever she wants. 'I know all about your afternoon in the garden - '

'Huh?' Do you know I had almost completely forgotten about that. I was so concerned about him being a potential wrecker, I had quite forgotten what I used to refer to as the Rape.

She giggled disarmingly. 'Did you really think he didn't know what was happening? Oh you are so *silly* sometimes!' She laughed happily, put an arm around my shoulders and led me to the garden bench. 'He fancied you from the moment he met you, did you know that? I'll bet he spent most of the time in the garden with his shirt off, right? - Yet he didn't dare approach you, happily married as he always thought you were...yes, I admit, that's his conservative streak.'

'I thought he was gay!'

'What? Good Lord, just because he was staying with Tom? He was just a lodger, though I suppose they must have seemed rather like husband and wife in public. Anyway, that's another proof that he's not *entirely* hidebound. He accepted Tom as a friend, without making any judgements about his lifestyle. They were good friends too, and I have no doubt whatsoever that they never *ever* went to bed together. Tom may have tried when they first met, but George made it clear he wasn't interested and they stayed friends.'

'I see,' I said, feeling a complete fool for having allowed myself to leap to wrong conclusions, something I do much too often.

'He told me the whole story soon after we met. He was ashamed and embarrassed about the whole thing, though he's still like a little boy who's had a great adventure, and I was the only one he trusted enough to tell...really Sally!' she said, mock-admonishing, 'you should know that sex and valium just don't mix!'

I allowed myself a small anxious laugh.

'He'd followed you into the kitchen and saw you grinding out the pills. Curious about your motives, he decided to play along. Tipped out his teacup on the hydrangeas while you weren't looking. Faked a drugged sleep...see?'

'That's so - embarrassing! How can I ever face him again!'

'Oh come on Sally.' Tammy said cheeringly, 'what's the big deal? You both enjoyed yourselves, didn't you? He said that being mounted by a woman was one of the great thrills of his life. That's the reason he told me! He wanted me to ride him the way you did! Probably his first experience of anything other than the missionary position!' She hooted with laughter.

And so did I, albeit self-consciously. 'And you've known this - '

'For ages!' she said, laughter chopping up her words. 'Oh I can just imagine it! You must have thought you'd finally - '

'Finally - !'

' - raped a man!!'

We were helpless with laughter, clinging on to each-other as if the other was the only way of holding onto reality, both remembering sultry late-night wide-awake conversations on our favourite subject, expressed in the phrase from My Fair Lady which we'd adapted, 'Why Can't a Woman...Rape a Man!' It became a catchphrase of ours, which we'd trot out in a Rex Harrison accent whenever a really good-looking man came into our purview. Eventually, just humming the tune would cause us to erupt with laughter.

And we sang it then, in exaggerated Harrison-voices, conducting ourselves gaily in the chilly wind. 'Why can't a woman/ Rape a man?/ Men are so awkward/ So eerily soft/ Men are so silly/ So easy to scan/ And it's trousersoff with any Wo - Man!'

Silly silly silly. Silly Sally silly Tammy.

Twenty years younger.

...but only for the moment.

'Wal, ain't that purty!' We looked up from our hilarity, gulped like schoolgirls caught smoking in the toilets, at Sam, standing hands-in-pockets, leaning against the screen-door. 'You girls are just like sisters, know that? I kin never understand the way girls love each-other. If men tried it they'd get arrested!'

'Pum pa pa pum pum, pum pa *pum*?' Tammy hummed, causing more shrieks of mad laughter. Tears were rolling down our cheeks. Sam grinned, shook his head, went upstairs to fix the balcony.

*

I asked Tammy if she loved George. 'Nearly,' she said. 'I wanted to love him, in fact I really thought I *should*. I found it hard. He's far too demanding, wants to dominate all the time.'

'Chauvinist.'

'I suppose so.'

'Lucky escape for me, then!'

'You said it!' she said vehemently. 'He is a prig. I have to admit it. *And* a Tory...'

'My God, so is Graham!'

'Yuk. What a fate for nice Socialist English roses. Anyway, what I was going to say is...'

'What?'

'If George decides to blow the gaff, I have no real objection to - disposing of him.'

'Disposing?' I said, eyes widening.

'Yah,' Tammy said in a Brooklyn voice. 'Shklit!' and she drew a finger across her throat.

*

George had gone for a walk all the way to the local shopping mall, a good two miles away. He returned enthusing about the price of Levi jeans. 'Twenty four dollars, can you believe it? That's around fourteen pounds. Do you know what they cost in the UK? More than twice that! I'd bet you couldn't get a pair in the King's Road in London for less than thirty-five pounds. That's *pounds*! ' He was flushed with exertion and excitement. 'Those crooks in England must be making massive profits. It's disgusting!'

'So why didn't you buy a pair?' Tammy asked provocatively.

'They didn't have my size, it's so disappointing. 30 waist ok, but not the length. Not one.'

'Tut tut tut,' Tammy shook her head sympathetically. 'Tut tut tut. Anyway, you'll have to live with the disappointment, won't you. And come with me. We have to talk.' With that she led him off, he still muttering about the immorality of the international garment trade.

Leaving me time to get washed and dressed.

*

I was interrupted in my getting dressed by a Peeping Sam. He had been out on the balcony of my bedroom working when I began to undress. I sincerely believe that he was genuinely embarrassed. At heart he is a gentleman - whatever that is. Because when I heard a noise from outside the screen door and looked up from pulling on my tights, he was standing abashed at the railing, masking-tape obscuring his eyes.

'Kin I look now? Are you finished?'

The man has a sense of humour. I laughed. 'Take that off,' I commanded, 'it's safe to peep now.'

He ripped the tape from his face gaily, unconcerned - as a macho man should be - at the removal of quite a few hairs from his eyebrows.

'I'm really sorry Sal, I was working out here, didn't realise you was in there undressing and all till it was too darn late. I didn't look, I promise.'

'You're a gentleman,' I said.

'It's kinda lucky, though, 'cos I want to have a talk with you, you listening?'

'Go on,' I said.

'Look, I been thinking about all this here. What Tammy told me an all. I want to help you Sally, honestly. Any way I can, see? When Tammy told me these guys got the stuff to cure you and won't even let you try it... I got mad. Really mad.'

'We don't know it'll cure me,' I said. 'It hasn't been tested properly on people yet. They have no idea about toxicity or anything - '

'Sal, I don't give a damn about toxiwhatsis. Hell, and you shouldn't neither! What the hell, if you're gonna die without it, - gee mam, I'm real sorry I said that. But you know what I mean. If it's your only hope - '

'Thank you Sam. Thank you for your friendship. ' I smiled, held out a hand which he shook far too gently - just

218

the way most people do, when they know I have cancer, as if I'm easily broken.

'Gee, that's ok .... so tell me what you want me to do.'

'Hm,' I said thoughtfully, giving him a gentle smile. 'All right Sam, you're in the team. Now, what do you know about safecracking?'

'Safecracking?' His eyes widened and a huge grin split his boyish face. 'Heck, learned it at my mamma's breast!'

'Jolly good!' I said.

'You know, I *love* that accent. Do you think you could make me happy and say that again?'

CHAPTER TWO

We met in the kitchen at 1am. I had (successfully!) slipped our hosts and George 15 mg of valium each, and they were all snoring merrily upstairs.

Sam was let in. He had arrived promptly, tapped on the window. Had there been any of the neighbours awake (MOST unlikely in Spireslea at that time!) they would have thought we were merely having an innocent wife-swapping party.

Everybody reported themselves ready.

'Up and ready to go,' She said, with a mock salute. 'My small fifth-columnist will be waiting, access will go as smooth as possible.'

'Maps,' I said, spreading them out on the table. 'Routes marked!'

'Tools at the ready surr!' Sam said, opening his bag which bulged with dangerous implements.

'Keys appropriated as requested!' Tammy said, waving C & B's Chevrolet keys in the air.

'Let's go!' M-D said.

*

We piled out of the house into the Chev. Sam drove. Through the deep-night streets, deserted except for the odd carload of Jesuit-college students coming home after a binge, and the occasional bored patrolling police car.

Two women, a little girl, a man in a Stetson and cowboy boots. (Carrying a grin of criminally mischievous proportions, he looked like a necrophiliac at the scene of a massacre. He had a revolver which he displayed proudly for us just before we set off. 'A man's got to be prepared for anything in this kind of game,' he said.)

We parked two blocks away from the Hospital. 'You ladies stay here, keep the engine running,' Sam said.

'No way!' I shrugged off his order. 'If you think I'm going to sit here while you - '

'Now hold on, hold on there!' Sam said, 'there's too many people here as it is - '

'We "wimmin" won't be coddled! We're coming!' Tammy said firmly.

'Dammit, why all my life I'm ordered about by females - Come on then, let's get going.'

As we arrived at the Lab building, it clicked open, quietly and smoothly. 'What kept you?' Kirsty asked, motioning us anxiously inside.

'Hello little warrior,' M-D said, giving her a quick kiss.

'Aw, slush!' the girl said, pushing her off. 'Come on, get in!'

The door closed behind us and Sam switched on his torch. 'Where's Security?' he asked nervously.

'He's sleeping good,' the child smiled behind her mask and winked. Then, 'Well come on, let's go!'

We slipped silently down the corridor to the door of the lab with its pompous sign proclaiming 'Dr Christopher Sloane. Authorised Personnel Only.'

Sam stared at the code-key lock. 'Heck,' he whispered. 'Never had none of these in my day!'

My heart sank. 'Can you do it?' I asked.

'Kin I do it?' Sam echoed, 'Kin I do it...' He punched a few numbers at random. Nothing happened.

A deep tiredness fell on me like a cloud. This was all so silly, I felt. This whole adventure was no more than the wishful thinking of a dying fool.

I sat on the floor, back against the wall.

'Hey, this aint no time to go flipflop on me,' Sam said, annoyed with himself. 'Shit damn!' he said, slapping the panel with the flat of his hand.

The door clicked open. 'See?' he said triumphantly, trying not to sound surprised, 'Told you I could do it!'

'Well done, ' I said cynically, dragging myself up.

'Feelin ok?' He asked. 'This is no time to get sick.'

'I'm fine,' I lied.

We entered the room and switched on the light. There it all was, the gleaming microscopes in their polythene covers. Slides, test-tubes, benches. The refrigerator with its frigid trapped death. Files higgledy-piggledy on sagging shelves.

The safe in a corner, under a bench. 'Here we go,' Sam said, taking a small wodge of plastique out of a polythene bag. He taped the stuff carefully onto the combination lock, and pinched it into a pyramid shape. Then he attached a wire, which he unrolled and twisted onto the terminals of a battery.

'We need a blanket now,' he said.

'I'll get one!' Kirsty offered, all brimming with excitement. She was thoroughly enjoying all this.

She returned in seconds, a light hospital blanket as big as herself embraced by her thin arms.

Sam draped the blanket over the safe. 'Let's get outta here!' he ordered.

We crouched outside the door. Sam pushed a switch. Whoom! A muffled thud.

Then we went into the room, opened the shattered safe.

Sam grinned, wallowing in his cleverness. I expected him to whoop, and he didn't hold it back. 'Whoo hoo! I done it!'

*

It was only after we had piled into the car - in a shaking mass of victory and relief, a Team of triumph, a happy band of Robbing Hoods - that we realised that George was sitting on the back seat, with a pistol.

'Welcome back,' he said. 'Now, driver, take us to the Police Station!' And the bastard laughed. 'Come on,' he said, 'start the engine!'

'George!' Tammy cried, 'How the hell did you get here?'

'In your boot!' He said, with triumph. 'When I tasted my coffee tonight, I knew your mad friend was up to her tricks again, that tonight would be the night. So I got this - ' he brandished the pistol - 'And climbed into the boot.'

'You're wrong, George, you're wrong!' Tammy erupted. 'You wouldn't shoot us. You love me!'

'So what if I do. There are more important things in this world than love! *You're* the ones that are wrong, this is all so crazy! And trying to drug me as well. Why shouldn't I shoot you? You're criminals, after all.'

'You're a pompous *prick*, George!' Tammy said bitterly.

'You never objected to it before,' he said. 'I thought you quite liked my prick. You and your *friend*,' he added, giving me a bitter look.

A light *ftoom*. George slumped forward. 'Hell mam, I had to do that.', Sam said, his revolver still smoking in his hand.

*

And in the morning, the horror of George's death still hanging over us, we had to act completely normal. Sam arrived at eight as usual. Started work as if nothing had happened. M-D and I both slept late, we had to - but C & B were used to us doing this. And they drove off to work ... 'phoned us at 11 to tell us the Horrible News.

'Hell Sally!' Barbara's tone mixed thrill and horror. 'Have *we* had a drama!'

'What?' I asked, beckoning M-D away from her cornflakes. She came over, sat herself on the arm of the chair in which I was sitting, still in my dressing-gown. Sam looked over from the window he was replacing.

'What's happened?' I asked.

'We've had a burglary! A heist! They've broken into the safe!'

'Good heavens. What's missing?'

'They've stolen the first batch of the compound, and all my lab notes...'

'That's terrible! I said. M-D clutched my shoulder, leaned forward in an attempt to hear. 'Who did it? How?'

'I don't know who,' she said, 'It could be anyone. Real professionals. It could be any one of our rivals. People would *kill* for this compound. The police are everywhere.'

'Any clues?' I asked.

'Who knows? They're interrogating everybody. It won't do any good though.'

'Who? Why?' I asked, heart skipping a beat.

'Well, Chris' paper is about to be published anyway. We have copies of everything. It's easy enough to make up another batch of the compound. It's going to be a race, that's for sure!'

Phew. 'How exciting!'

So all that remained was for us to keep our cool until the Saturday, and then to step into the 'plane with tearful farewells.

GOODBYE America...

POSTSCRIPT

I don't know whether the compound is working or not. I do feel quite a lot better. I'm carefully following the dosages recommended in Barbara's notes. So is Kirsty, whose hair has grown back and looks like any healthy six-year old over there, playing on the beach with M-D, who too seems to be blossoming into a cheerful, happy teenager, full of light and bright and charm.

It'll take some time for the various authorities to figure out that we were to blame for the theft; that we didn't go on to London from Houston, but stepped into an Air Varig jet instead, under assumed names, and flew off to Rio.

Sam - who has just gone to get me an ice cream (we've become lovers, by the way. His body is soft and strong and fit for a fifty-year old man. I'm beginning to love him.) - assures me that George will never be found. Never. Though he refuses to give any further information on this...

Tammy sits over there, head bowed. I know she misses George, and isn't really happy. I'd bet she'll be going home soon.

To what?

Ah well, have a Pina Collada...

That couple further down the beach look maddeningly familiar... could it be Joan and Harry?

THE AUTHOR

Jon Elkon was born and brought up in Apartheid South Africa. His parents were committed in a bourgeois way, to the struggle against Apartheid. His father Sam was a member of the Industrial Council, as well as being a self-made mattress millionaire and a member of the Industrial Council. As such he worked for the recognition of black trade unions. Mother Valerie, as a member of the Black Sash women's movement, protested against the injustices of the system by standing mutely in public places in a black sash symbolising the death of democracy.

At 20 he escaped. Arriving in the UK penniless and homeless, he spent time on the streets, sleeping in shop doorways and parks. He was eventually rescued by the kindness of friends.

These adventures are the basis for his trilogy *Umfaan's Heroes, Laszlo's Millions* and *Celine*, the first two of which were published by Andre Deutsch almost twenty years after the events they lie about. His first was received enthusiastically by the critics. *Umfaan's Heroes* has now been re-issued by the Author in a new paperback edition and the sequel, *Laszlo's Millions*, has been fully remastered and rewritten – Elkon asserts it "rewrites 1970's London" and is also available in paperback.

Jon Elkon now teaches in an inner city school in London, writes occasionally prizewinning poetry and novels.

He has one son, Jamie, who lives in Cape Town and wonderful grandchildren all over the place.

Made in the USA
Columbia, SC
22 December 2017